GRAND THEFT N.Y.E.

HEIST HOLIDAYS

KATRINA JACKSON

For Kai
Enjoy this mess!

CONTENT WARNINGS

Mentions of parental illness and death

MAY

ONE

THE EXCLUSIVE KISMET Diamonds Kentucky Derby afterparty was just the kind of decadent, ridiculous rich white people event Cleo loved. Some people with her background fretted for weeks about what to wear and how to do their hair, hoping they could sneak into the ultra-exclusive party without incident. She'd seen it happen more than once but it was always easy to find other people like her, the ones who didn't belong.

Sometimes she felt sorry for them. She'd pick them out in their outfits that cost more than some people's annual rent — their clothes always tasteful but boring — and know they'd paid a stylist a small fortune to dress them to blend in, and still they'd stick out. Not because they were wearing the wrong clothes or had too little money, but because they were so worried about not fitting in... that they didn't.

Watching those misfits taught Cleo that it wouldn't ever matter what she wore or what accent she affected because she'd always stick out like a sore thumb, so she stopped giving a damn.

Sometimes she pitied the people who had yet to realize how freeing it could be not to care what anyone with too much money in their bank accounts thought about you. She couldn't imagine going through life hoping to be accepted by people who weren't better, just richer. It sounded lonely. And pathetic. And that wasn't her MO at all. So when she stepped out of her cream Mercedes Benz truck in front of the rented mansion in the hills for the Kismet VIP party and handed her key to the valet, all eyes were on her, because where else would they be? She was a five-foot ten-inch thick bitch with a size eleven shoe and an ass that made grown adults' mouths water; fitting in would be a tragedy when she looked this good. As she walked up the rose-pink carpet toward the front door, she knew there wouldn't be anyone at this party who looked like her; not by a long shot.

The mistake she'd watched a whole bunch of new money people make was to try to fit in when the wave was really just to pretend to be too good to be around these degenerate rich fucks. And Cleo definitely didn't have to pretend on that front because she really was too good to be in a room with these people. And she channeled that certainty into a haughty, but slightly amused, stare as she handed over her invitation.

It was fake. Like really fucking fake.

She and her team had planned to intercept an invitation. They'd been planning this job for a year and had marked their target; someone whose life was too chaotic to realize their invitation to the gaudy new money set event of the year hadn't arrived until it was too late to matter. What they hadn't been able to plan for was their mark getting picked up and charged on sixteen counts of arson the week before invitations went out. You truly could never tell with the wealthy and ridiculous.

There hadn't been enough time to choose and stake out a new target before invitations arrived, so her team had had to scramble. Their forger, Alex, had done her best to recreate the invitation based on past designs and the #KismetKYDerby hashtag on Instagram. But at the end of the day, they'd been running blind, and this was the moment of truth.

The security guard looked at the invitation, shined a blue light flashlight over it. Then his eyes wandered lazily from Cleo's eyes down her body and back again. "Name."

"Jessica Hare," she said without an ounce of mirth, even though she and her hacker Brian had laughed for a solid hour when they'd added her to tonight's guest list.

The security guard pulled out his tablet.

This was where amateurs usually fucked themselves. Pretty much all security guards are hired because they're big, look mean, probably are mean, and are good at looking at people with nothing but suspicion and hostility in their eyes; they were big, dumb intimidation machines.

But just because the big motherfucker with the wicked scar across his left eyebrow was outside of an event that probably cost millions to throw, didn't mean he was necessarily any better than the bouncers at her favorite hip-hop club growing up. And what she'd learned from those lecherous jackasses was that big tits, a big ass, and a slightly parted mouth was more than enough to get them to overlook a sketchy driver's license – or in this case a just alright forgery – and let you inside the venue.

"Enjoy your night, ma'am," the security guard said, extending his arm to hand her invitation back to her.

"Thank you," Cleo responded, making sure to let just the tip of her acrylic nail trail across his index finger. She watched as his right eye ticked, and his gaze narrowed on her breasts. "You do the same."

She turned and walked from the security checkpoint to the front door. Another security guard pulled the door open for her and she smiled at him as she passed.

"I'm in," she whispered just loud enough for her earpiece to pick up her voice.

"Of course you are, we're not amateurs," Brian said.

"Shut up," Alex hissed.

Cleo smiled at Alex's voice. If there was a good cop-bad cop dynamic on this crew, Cleo was absolutely the former and Alex was a bad cop and drill sergeant rolled into one. If she said radio critical, they all knew it meant stay off the airwaves unless absolutely necessary and no one dared cross her. Not even Cleo. Usually. But this wasn't the time to needle her crew, not when they were so close. And not on a night when Cleo's job was really so simple.

Just getting in the house was half the battle.

The other half... Well, that was sitting across the wide ballroom on a raised dais where the VIPs of all VIPs were playing a high stakes poker game. "Let's get this bag," she whispered to herself and her crew and stepped gingerly into the #KismetDerbyExperience ready to do what she'd always done best: rob a rich man for all he was worth.

Cleo had seen this mansion from as many angles as possible. She and Alex had pored over the blueprints on file with the city, the *Architectural Digest's* spread when it was built, and every picture they could find from parties thrown here over the years. But as often happened when her research met her con jobs, she was shocked for a minute at how ugly it all was in person.

The room was supposed to look like an ancient

Roman villa, and Cleo had to work double time to stop from frowning at the fake columns around the room, the gaudy fountains scattered around the perimeter and the fake cobbling on the dance floor. It was good awful and Cleo made sure to commit it all to memory so she never forgot the most important lesson of her vocation: rich people are dumb as fuck with their money!

"Stop judging the interior design," Alex said in her ear.

"But—"

"Money," she hissed before Cleo could launch into a diatribe. And she was right.

She stopped walking and turned in a circle. There were couches and settees all over the room, clustered around the semi-precious gem art Kismet was touring around the country at these parties. The traveling art exhibit was an incredibly expensive excuse to get rich people together to... do rich people things, she guessed.

Cleo had originally considered trying to steal a few of the art pieces. She could only imagine how much she'd get for the intact sculptures in the Middle East. Even just hacking them apart and selling them individually would be a decent payday. But Kismet security was something serious. And why choose the hardest road when there was an easier path to plunder? At least in this version of the plan, she got to dress up.

When she'd seen this specific dress in Saks, she hadn't known when she'd need it, but she knew she would. As soon as she'd run the pads of her fingers over the nearly see-through bodice of the trashiest expensive dress in the store, she could imagine it on her body. For a fleeting moment, she pictured herself wearing it on a date, like a real date, not a job, but she'd pushed that image out of her mind and imagined distracting a slightly jowly banker with her breasts while her hands plugged a virus on a USB stick into his computer behind his back. She was more comfortable with the latter scenario. And now that the time had come, she was happy she'd had this dress on deck.

There was something so wonderful about walking through a party like this in a dress that was barely a suggestion and definitely an advertisement. Hell, it might even, technically, be lingerie since it was made up of equal parts see-through lace and slinky jersey that just barely covered her good bits but gave a clear indication of everything underneath as she moved. A dress like this made her feel powerful and not at all as if she fit in.

It wasn't that she couldn't blend in if the job called for it, but her specialty was understanding how to get the crowd to focus on her. If a moment called for all eyes on the decoy, she was the woman for the job because Cleo – unlike Alex – didn't have a problem grabbing a room by the balls. And she always made sure to hold on tight until her crew had cleared the place out around them and were on their way to safety. There were few people of any gender who could do that better than her.

As she turned in a slow circle, looking down her broad nose at the people around her, she knew she'd gotten their attention without even really trying. When she resumed walking toward the poker table, she put in a concentrated effort to make sure all eyes were on her on purpose. She smiled and smirked and sometimes even winked at men ogling her too hard, just for the fun of pissing off their wives. She reveled in her own audacity, which only made everyone else angrier. Her ego soaked up every drop of their annoyance like water. This was why she was one of the best — if not THEE best — at this kind of job: conning wasn't work to Cleo, it was her calling.

"Champagne, ma'am?" a waiter asked her.

She smiled and plucked a flute from the tray in their hand. She didn't need to flip the silver disc to know that it would be engraved with the Tiffany's symbol and she didn't need to see the tag on the waiter's uniform to know it was Gucci; it was her job to know. Besides, like most of these lavish parties for the disgustingly wealthy, name brands were everywhere, right on down to the $15,000 fur rug she was stepping on with her $45 Perspex heels.

Cleo brought the glass to her lips and took a small sip, the only indulgence she'd allow herself tonight since she never mixed liquor with work. As she savored the flavor of the best champagne money could buy, she turned in another full circle, ostensibly toying with the room again, but really making sure the pieces of art her team had identified for removal were present and accounted for on the walls around the room. When she was satisfied that all was as it should be, she winked at an older woman and her younger wife who looked like they wanted to do more than stare, before turning confidently toward her target.

It was time to get down to business.

She found him exactly where she expected, at the poker table surrounded by other old, drunk, lecherous men just like him. Francis Pugh III technically owned the house where Kismet was ringing in the end of the Kentucky Derby, but that was a temporary reality. Cleo and her team knew he was no more than three months from losing it all. The SEC was investigating him for insider trading; his soon-to-be ex-wife had a team of private investigators looking for money she was certain he was hiding in the Bahamas; and unless he got an influx of cash soon, the bank was going to foreclose on this house before the end of the year.

As far as Cleo was concerned, Frank was the best kind of target. His financial situation was so precarious and the veil maintaining his veneer of wealth so thin that any cop or insurance investigator would be stupid not to look at him as the possible perpetrator when he filed a police report because his entire house had been cleaned out overnight. And if a dumb cop was inclined to believe him, Cleo knew she could count on Frank's ex-wife to set them straight and make sure all the heat of an investigation went right back to him. By the time anyone cleared Frank of suspicion in the eyes of the law — but never in the eyes of his wife — Cleo and her crew would be long gone. And, to add another wonderful layer of useful ignorance, not many people trying to solve the case of a high-tech heist would give a second thought to the too tall, nearly naked Black woman in the expensive dress, cheap heels, and fire engine red wig.

All Cleo had to do was focus and keep her eyes on the prize — the balding man with a fat cigar hanging from his lips — and this job would keep her and her crew set for months. And as it happened, focus was easy for Cleo when money was involved.

It was why she slowed down as she ascended the stairs. She wanted to feel every second of this moment, to see when he saw her; when his mouth went slack, his lit cigar drooped, and his eyes widened. He looked like a terrible 90's Wall Street movie; even more reason to rob him blind. She took each step up the dais with deliberate care so Frank had enough time to drink in her curves, to imagine running his sweaty hands over them, to fantasize about her body over his in bed. She wanted Frank and everyone at the table to wonder who she was and become desperate to have her hanging from their arm for the rest of the night. This, too, was a thing she'd learned early: dangling a jewel in front of greedy eyes was a better sleight of hand than an explosion.

Cleo walked toward Frank, her eyes never leaving his. She gave him the impression that she only had eyes for him, even as she clocked her surroundings in her peripheral vision.

When she was by his side, he practically pushed the woman perched on the arm of his chair to the ground.

"Hey," the woman whined as she stumbled in last season's Jimmy Choo patent leather platform heels.

Now in her normal life, Cleo would have offered to help the girl slash Frank's tires, but she was an actress — of a sort — and couldn't afford to even let her eyes fall on the other woman while she was in character as the kind of woman who'd find Frank's gross behavior attractive and flattering. She simply moved past her and settled onto the now unoccupied arm of Frank's chair. She let her hip rest against his shoulder heavily, just enough pressure for him to feel how soft she was, knowing that his imagination would handle the rest.

"What do you say, sweetheart?" he asked, showing his hand to her.

Cleo glanced at his cards. They were terrible.

He was going to lose no matter what, probably. She could have told him to fold, but in her experience, men like him didn't want advice from women. So many men hated a woman with opinions — rich or poor — that Cleo had learned not to bother giving any of her actually great advice while on a job. Never mind what well-meaning people said in fake deep poems or inspirational blogs, it was more than emotionally satisfying to watch an asshole fall, *especially* when you saw it coming from a mile away. Besides, Cleo's job wasn't to give her marks her true self. She had to give them what they wanted at all times so they'd let their guards down.

So instead of answering Frank's question, she leaned into his side, pressed her left breast into his shoulder and giggled. She didn't even need to speak. Just a light, effervescent tinkle that made insecure men feel big and strong. Insecure men like Frank.

He smiled at her cleavage, shifted in his seat — probably to hide his erection — and threw a few cards on the table.

She looked at his hand again. Those weren't the cards she might have discarded, but whatever, she didn't care if he won or lost a little bit of money right now since he was about to lose it all in a few hours.

"Final bets," the dealer called.

While the men considered their new hands, Cleo took the opportunity to look around the table, not because she cared but because she was always on the lookout for more work. A hustler never slept. All of the men around the table looked like Frank, honestly; maybe a little older or younger, but definitely rich, gaudy, and bleary-eyed from alcohol. Easy targets. They didn't inspire her in the moment, but she catalogued their faces and made a mental note to have Brian get their identities. She could always rob them next year.

She dismissed each man in turn until her eyes landed on the tall drink of water sitting directly across from her. The minute her eyes landed on him, Cleo felt... something. While the other men were slouched over their hands, a piece of young arm candy perched on the arms of their chairs, this man was the only one sitting alone, back straight and focused. He was also the only person not trying to angle his head to look up her dress. Sure, his eyes darted from the cards in his hand to the crease of her thighs, so it wasn't like he was ignoring her — and she would have been offended if he was — but he hadn't been swept away by her. There was something intriguing about a man so in control of himself that she couldn't fully distract him.

She didn't like it, but she did find it interesting.

The tall Asian man's long hair reached just past his shoulders and the faint shadow of his beard made him look slightly disheveled and maybe even a bit dangerous. Cliché on top of clichés, but Cleo was into the look. A lot. But it was his long, thick fingers that made her do something she never did while working; she momentarily lost focus. One minute she was casing the poker table and the next minute she was running her teeth along her bottom lip, imagining the man's fingers playing with the strip of her thong between her ass cheeks. She looked up and her eyes clashed with his.

His face was even better full on. Sharp nose. Intense dark eyes. And a calm that made her shiver. Especially when Frank's unhinged anger interrupted the heat of that silent moment between Cleo and the stranger. She looked down at him dispassionately and remembered that she was here to work, not ogle the locals.

She leaned away from Frank as he yelled and gesticulated wildly at a man who looked like he could be his son, spittle flying from his mouth. The other man yelled back. Cleo understood enough of the exchange to assume they were each accusing the other of cheating.

She huffed a laugh and shook her head in judgment. Rich people were always so worried about people stealing from them, but never when it counted. Not when a woman Interpol had once called an international menace was sitting right next to them. Idiots.

But whatever, she thought to herself. Karma was a bitch and Cleo was happy AF to be her weapon.

The fight was, loud and wet as it happened to be, was more than a little convenient. Now that all eyes weren't on her, she wiggled her right index finger under the thick bracelet on her left wrist. It looked like a gaudy piece of jewelry — and it was — but it also hid a device that Brian had rigged to pull information from any chipped debit and credit cards nearby, as well as clone cell phone internet browser data. It was Cleo's favorite tool; hands off but effective. The only problem was that the device's range was small. To make it work, Cleo had to get *very* close, but she was great at that.

Frank jabbed his hands at the other man, and Cleo's eyes caught on a signet ring on his left hand with at least a carat of diamonds and a Cartier watch on his right wrist. She frowned, knowing how many new purses those two pieces of jewelry might buy, but also knowing that she'd have to leave them behind. She'd cut her teeth as a good pickpocket, but she'd never been that good.

She pressed the tiny button to activate Brian's device, inched her wrist was as close to Frank's body as possible, and pretended to care why these two grown men were yelling at one another like children as she waited.

"Got it," Brian said through the receiver in her ear three very long minutes later.

"Get out of there," Alex added.

Cleo's eyes lifted to the ballroom, accidentally

making eye contact with one of the waiters across the room. Alex was great at staying calm and in control while they were working. She was a natural in the field. Her eyes didn't betray any anxieties or fear. She usually looked bored. But Cleo recognized the urgency in her gaze because no one knew her little sister's micro-expressions better than her.

They were all a team, but Cleo and Alex had been a team since Alex was in diapers and once they'd started boosting, their dynamics had been set, never changing; Cleo set up the job and prepped the room, and Alex swept in to close it out. Whether it was a few boxes of Hamburger Helper or a house full of art, she and her sister were the same.

And now Cleo's part in this whole play was done.

"Cleo, move," Brian said.

She nodded once, barely moving her head. Alex nodded back, and smiled as she offered a tray of champagne to a woman who couldn't even be bothered to acknowledge the human being holding the tray out to her.

She stood from the chair.

Frank didn't notice. He was too busy yelling at the other man. Still, Cleo was happy to get away from him as quickly as possible, he seemed like the clingy, slobbering drunk type and he wasn't worth nearly enough for all that hassle.

She spared a quick glance at the man across the

table. His head was bowed as the man next to him whispered in his ear. Cleo frowned briefly but turned to walk confidently away from the poker table as if the argument behind her wasn't getting louder and louder. She cut a determined but slow path through the ballroom.

It was important to always leave a party at a slower pace than you entered. Amateurs ran. People who felt guilty ran. Cleo was far from an amateur, and no one needed as much money as the people in this room hoarded; guilt wasn't in her repertoire.

She smiled at the security guards again and walked back to the valet. She hadn't been at the party long, but it was noticeably colder outside. She handed over her ticket and wished she'd worn just a little more clothing. Cleo wrapped her arms around her body and shivered.

"Would you like to borrow my jacket?"

She turned quickly at the deep voice she instinctively knew was aimed at her. The man from the poker table was standing in front of her, his suit coat clutched in his right hand and extended toward her. It had been so long since Cleo had felt shock — real shock, not the artifice she used to elicit arousal or interest from a man she was just about to scam.

She smiled at him — a real smile — but shook her head. "No, but thank you."

"Are you sure?" he asked, stepping just a bit closer.

She gestured toward the valet. "My car has heat. I'll be fine in a few minutes."

"Your car, Mr. Shimizu," another valet said.

He'd never handed over a ticket.

They both turned to the curb, and she lifted an eyebrow at what looked to be a pristine vintage gray Jaguar E-Type.

"Series one? Roadster?" she asked.

"Good eye," he said, the hand with his coat dropping to his side.

Cleo noticed things. Again, that was her job. And one of the things that had always fascinated her was the way real money and power moved in the world. Frank was rich but didn't have real money or power. Even if her team wasn't about to take everything he had; his wife, the bank, the federal government...someone would have soon enough, because he was careless with it. He knew it was a fleeting thing. He'd accumulated a little money and then done what most people did; he frittered it away on lavish vacations, gifts for his wife and mistresses, expensive meals to impress people who hated him, and so many bad investments. His money was as short as his stature and his power was as precarious as his wedding vows. Frank was the kind of man Cleo liked to rob; someone whose grasp on their money was as flimsy as a cheap synthetic wig.

But this man was different. The way he carried himself said it all. His money was longer than his dick, she could feel it in her bones. She licked her lips. If he'd made his money, it had only been to add to the kind of generational wealth Cleo couldn't even imagine, and his power was probably the kind Frank had wet dreams about. Everything from the way he stood to the easy way he stared at her – as if he knew she would come around to taking his jacket soon enough – identified him as the kind of man who was used to getting his way. The world spun on his axis, never the other way around.

Sometimes Cleo hesitated to target men like him. They could be dangerous. But that was exactly what made her lick her lips as she looked at him, her eyes traveling down his long body.

"Would you like to warm yourself in my car while you wait?" he asked.

She raised her eyes to his and then turned her head to look at his car. The top was down. "The heaters on that car aren't great. I'd be warmer staying right where I am."

He ducked his head and his mouth spread into a thin smile. The move was surprisingly endearing.

"You might be right," he acceded.

"I usually am."

"But the whole point of a car like this isn't to stay warm."

Cleo couldn't help but laugh. But not that girlish giggle she used on marks. This laugh was in her regular deep voice, and it came from her belly, rather than her throat. "It's not?"

Mr. Shimizu's eyes widened. "No," he said, stepping forward again. "The point of a car like this is to throw the top down and freeze in the wind while you push it and yourself to your limits. You want to drive it so fast, even the concept of a speed limit doesn't exist. The cold is worth it."

Cleo had inched toward him as he spoke. They were just close enough to touch each other. Any other man at that table would have already tried to grope her by now. But he hadn't. And she more than liked that.

"So you like speed?" she asked.

He huffed a laugh and dipped his head forward, his mouth closer to hers. "I like to live life to the fullest. Sometimes that means I like to go fast." He stepped forward again, pressing himself and the firm mound of his erection against her. "And sometimes that means I like to go slow."

"I don't like slow," Cleo said.

"I didn't think you would," he said with a small chuckle. "Come home with me."

It wasn't quite a request or a command, but his voice was a deep smooth burr that inched under the thin fabric of her dress and caressed her skin, and her body responded. Her nipples began to tingle as they hardened; her mouth went dry as all the moisture in her body headed south to her pussy. She wanted this man. More than she could remember wanting anyone in years. Maybe ever.

But he was so rich, and in Cleo's experience, rich men — even sexy ones — were better at seduction than actual sex. They were too selfish, too cocky, and very comfortable letting their money hit all the spaces inside their partners their dicks couldn't reach.

So really, Cleo thought momentarily, she could just rob him instead. The money from selling his belongings on the black market would probably keep her satisfied longer than his stroke, she thought.

But then Cleo did something she'd never done before. She second-guessed herself. Did she want to fuck him more than rob him? Her brain appraised the car and the disheveled Tom Ford suit with the diamond cufflinks, guessing she could probably take herself on a cute little girl's trip at the end of the summer with those. But her pussy was practically weeping at his long fingers and broad shoulders and shy but somehow still confident smile; all parts of his body that would look amazing between her legs.

And in the end, for the first time ever, her pussy won out.

Cleo had been robbing men since she was a pre-teen trying to get enough money to feed herself and Alex after their dad had practically wasted away in the wake of their mom's sudden death. She hadn't had time for emotions. Emotions wouldn't put a happy meal in front of her sister at night. It wouldn't get them school uniforms, or shoes good enough to stop the other kids from teasing them. Emotions didn't pay the bills when your dad was too grief stricken to write checks.

But the longer she was in the business, the more obvious it had become that, while money solved a myriad of problems, it didn't fuck her to sleep and hold her tight at night.

"Take me for a ride," she whispered against his lips.

TWO

CLEO HAD BEEN in plenty of expensive fast cars with rich men. If there was a rich man archetype, it had to be "wastes money on a car they'd dreamt about as a kid," and it was usually #boringAF. Just a rich man-child with a shiny, costly new toy. Been there, stole that. But from the minute Mr. Shimizu opened his car door for her, his lanky body bent nearly half over, two fingers casually holding the car handle and his eyes searing into hers as he waited patiently for her to walk to the curb, nothing about this ride had been like all the others. He wasn't like all the other men she'd met before, and that, at least, burned away some of the guilt she felt at leaving a job half-finished. That, and the way she felt when he slid into the driver's seat and turned his key in the ignition.

"Are you ready?" he practically growled at her.

Cleo shivered, but not because of the cold. "Let's go."

He nodded and turned to ease the car down the winding driveway back toward the main road.

Based on their plan, Marcus and Gina were probably prepping any small items their fences had requested for transport. In about three hours, when the crowd had begun to thin — or pass out — they'd start the heavy lifting. The security for the party, while big and intimidating, was provided by Kismet, not Frank, and their contract was to protect the company's sculptures, not Frank's possessions. Once they were gone, the house was as vulnerable as any other; maybe even more so, because Frank couldn't afford his own security anymore.

That was the beauty of the plan they'd spent an entire year crafting. Who would dare rob a house that had so recently been filled with hundreds of people and crawling with some of the best security in the world? Cleo and Alex and their crew, that's who.

As soon as Kismet's sculptures and security were gone, Alex would hand Frank his last drink of the night. It would be laced; he'd pass out and then the real work started. They'd snatch and pack away all the artwork he'd had recently appraised, the jewelry he was holding hostage from his wife because she'd dared to leave him, even some of the good silver. It'd take them no more than two hours — an hour and a half, if Alex had her way — and then they'd pack up their fake catering vans and scatter.

By the time Frank woke up the next morning, the vans would be in a different state, Alex and Brian would be on a plane to a different country and, according to the plan, Cleo would be on another plane to some place warm, all destinations unknown, just in case. And as Cleo settled into Mr. Shimizu's roadster, she did so with full knowledge that Brian was already cleaning out Frank's bank accounts. A job very well done.

As the car began to inch forward, she took the opportunity to slyly take her earpiece from her ear and shove it into her purse. She also sent Alex a quick text saying she would be MIA for a few hours. She'd never done this on a job before and she knew her sister would wild out when she saw it, but that wouldn't be for a few hours, and by then... Well, anything could have happened by then.

"What's your name?" she asked. "Your first name."

He turned onto the two-lane rural highway. It was so dark out here, not a streetlight to be found. All Cleo could see was the black asphalt of the road cut through with yellow and white lines, washed out by Mr. Shimizu's almost too bright headlights. On either side of the road, there seemed to be nothing but dark forest, tall trees looming over them and blotting out most of the sky. The further he drove, the more Cleo felt as if there was no one else in the world but the two of them. And she liked that more than she expected.

"Robert," he answered after a while.

"That's so... regular," she laughed, turning her head to look at him and confirm that there wasn't anything about him that seemed regular. At least not to her.

His lips barely moved but his eye crinkled at the corner. Even that simple move seemed extraordinary to her. "What should I call you?" he asked, glancing quickly at her and then back to the road.

Ah. So here was a moment that made dating hard. To give her real name or the alias she'd been using while throwing money around at the Derby? It was a conundrum. If Alex was here — she'd never have let Cleo get in the car; but if she were already in the car — Alex would have yelled at her to use her alias. But the thought of introducing herself to this man as Jessica Hare made her frown. The alias was a cute inside joke with her crew, but she wanted to hear this man say her name desperately. So, she decided to ignore the advice of her imaginary sister in her head.

"Cleo," she said. "Just Cleo." A girl's gotta have boundaries.

"Okay, Just Cleo. Buckle up and let me take you for that ride."

More than a few men had whispered a series of

explicit things they wished they could do to her; filthy promises their actions rarely lived up to. But not a single wet paragraph whispered into her harassed ears had ever turned her on as much as that simple sentence. She felt desire coil tight in her stomach as she reached behind her to grab the seat-belt, never taking her eyes from him.

"I'm gonna call you Mr. Shimizu," she said in her sultriest voice.

"Is that what's gonna get you off?"

Her thighs clenched at the lack of judgment in that question. His voice was full of nothing but curious interest, as if he was trying to figure her out as keenly as she was trying to understand him. "For starters," she whispered.

He grunted.

Cleo felt a small lag as he prepared to shift gears, moving his foot from the gas to the clutch. The back of his hand brushed her thigh as he moved the gear shift. They both jumped as the wind picked up, blowing her hair around in the air.

She hoped she'd glued it down tight enough.

Cleo crossed her right leg over her left — her already short dress riding dangerously high up her thighs — and smiled as his head darted to the right to take the sight in quickly.

"You should watch the road," she purred.

He smiled and turned to her. "Where's the fun in that?"

SOME PEOPLE TRIED to rationalize their grifts. They liked to tell themselves they stole just to put food on the table, or they created elaborate self-serving stories in their heads, casting themselves as Robin Hood types. Cleo didn't. Sure, she'd first started picking pockets and boosting from stores to feed herself and Alex, but she'd had a lot of friends back then who'd tried it, realized it wasn't for them and moved on. But Cleo hadn't, because she liked it. No, fuck that, she'd loved it. The thrill of the unknown, the danger of knowing they *could* get caught, the escape; she'd never known a rush like it.

But over the years, her excitement had begun to wane. Never make your passion your job, she'd heard someone say once, and she was just starting to feel it. There was so little joy these days in slipping a man's timepiece off his wrist while he looked her dead in the eyes, trying to seduce her. She could do it. She had done it. She'd started to suspect that she needed more, even though she wasn't ready to admit it to herself and certainly not ready to broach the topic with Alex.

But as Mr. Shimizu pushed the car one more mile over the speed limit and then another and another, Cleo felt something she hadn't felt in a long time: the exhilarating rush of so much dangerous possibility. By the time the small car closed in on one hundred miles an hour, she was squirming in her seat, her knees pressed so tight together she was worried she might strain a muscle. Her back arched from the seat. She wanted to feel the wind on her barely covered nipples. This feeling was new and different, and she let it take over.

Her head thrashed side to side in ecstasy as small orgasmic ripples began to radiate up from her clit to her stomach and the sensitive undersides of her breasts and down her thighs to her toes. Had a man ever gotten her off without touching her? Fuck no. Was she desperate to see what happened when Mr. Shimizu inevitably did? So much.

She moaned as her muscles relaxed and she slumped in her seat, her body momentarily over-loaded with excitement. Her head lolled to the side, and her gaze zeroed in on the dangerous combination of his big hand and long fingers wrapped around his gear shift and the very obvious bulge in his pants. This was the biggest rush of her life, and it had only just begun.

"Is this too fast for you?" He had to practically yell the words at her, but they still made her shiver.

"Not yet, Mr. Shimizu," she said, sounding confident but also nearly mad with lust, which was exactly how she felt.

"Good girl," he muttered just loud enough for her to hear.

Her eyes closed on those two words and she

started squirming in her seat again. She heard the gears shift and felt the car accelerate as she lost the battle to keep her knees together. The moan that fell from her lips was obscenely loud and she loved it.

"It's a good thing this seat is leather," she gasped, "it's going to be very wet soon."

"I wish I'd known that I might be in this situation," Mr. Shimizu said.

"Why?"

His eyes darted to her open legs. "I would have brought an automatic."

"You don't seem like the kind of man who owns one."

"Oh no, I do. Just one. It doesn't see much action, but this would have been worth pulling it out of storage." He licked his lips so she knew exactly what he was thinking, and now she was thinking about that too.

"If you had a free hand, what would you be doing with it right now?"

He didn't laugh or smile. When he turned to her, his face was serious and his eyes were full of dark intent. It made Cleo shiver. "If I had a hand to touch you, it'd be inside you already. Probably would have been before we even left the Estate."

That was all she needed to hear.

Cleo sank down in her seat, slipped her feet free of her shoes and lifted her right leg up, spreading herself open for him to see. She moved her hand to her inner thigh and caressed her skin.

"I'm happy to lend you a hand."

The car sped up just a bit more as her hand descended toward the warm depths between her legs. She groaned and circled her hips when the tips of her long nails scratched the crease of her leg. He didn't turn toward her, but she knew she had as much of his attention as was possible; maybe even a bit more than was safe.

She ran the pads of her fingers over the gusset of her underwear. "My panties are already soaked," she breathed.

"Then you should take them off." Such a polite command.

"Yes, sir, Mr. Shimizu."

He grinned.

It wasn't easy or particularly sexy to get her underwear over her ass and down her legs with the seatbelt still across her chest and waist while in a car built for someone at least five inches shorter than her, but she did it. And in life, completing the task was more important than making it pretty. At least that was Cleo's motto. Besides, Mr. Shimizu didn't seem to care, since his only response was to take his hand from the gear shift and hold it out to her.

She happily dropped the small wet scrap of fabric into his palm and then watched as he brought it to his nose. He sniffed it deeply and then stuffed it into his pants pocket before resting his hand on the gear shift again.

"You didn't seem like a freak at the poker table," she breathed wistfully.

"Then I guess my poker face is still intact. But you were the only person at that table I wanted to fuck, so I didn't have to hide it for long." He spoke to her in an easy rumble, his voice calm and nonchalant as if nothing untoward was going on. It was driving Cleo and her pussy over the edge. "Now, where were we?" he asked with an arched eyebrow.

"You were driving fast as hell and I was about to fuck myself with my hands. For you."

She felt the car speed up yet again.

"Is there anything else you want me do?" she asked, as she ran the pads of her fingers up and down her wet slit.

"Besides be as loud as possible?" He shook his head twice and then stopped. "Actually, yes." He downshifted the car to take a curve in the road, slower but still fast as fuck, and then sped up again. "I want you to tell me when you're close. I don't want you to come until I say so. Do we have a deal?"

Cleo should have been surprised, but she wasn't. Every rich man she'd ever conned or legitimately dated had wanted to take control of her in any way possible; whether it was what she wore, how she spoke or how they fucked. It was the kind of personality trait that came part and parcel with money and power and she always denied them that, even if it might get her the money she wanted faster. She was about to deny Mr. Shimizu that as well, but then he spoke again.

"I want you to tell me when you're close because I want to get you off myself. You can warm yourself up, but every time you come tonight, it'll be because I gave you exactly what you needed. Deal?"

Cleo moaned, which was the most enthusiastic yes she could imagine. It was also the only response she could give since, halfway through his declaration, she'd slipped two fingers inside herself.

"How wet are you?" he asked, as if this was the kind of thing he did regularly. Hell, maybe it was.

"Soaked."

"Warm?"

"So fucking hot," she corrected.

"Aching?"

"I'm not going to last long if you keep interrogating me while I fuck myself."

"How many fingers do you have in your pussy?"

"Oh god," she groaned. "Two."

"Add another."

She did.

"Are you touching your clit?" he asked.

"God, no," she gasped. "I'll come too quick. Fuck, I'm gonna come soon anyway."

"Don't," was all he said.

She shivered. "I'm not going to last," she groaned, the heel of her hand just brushing her hooded clit.

He didn't answer, but she felt the car slow in increments as she plunged her fingers in and out of herself. She alternated between fast and slow strokes, trying to stave off the inevitable. Her free hand was holding onto the car's center console for dear life, because what she wanted was to drag his hand to her pussy so he could touch her. But that was certainly dangerous, so she forced herself to wait.

"I'm so close," she panted in a strained voice.

"I know, sweetheart. Just give me a second," he said, his voice soothing and calm.

He pulled the car to a stop in a dirt runoff. Cleo whined as he put the car in park and then practically tore his seatbelt open.

Cleo fumbled to unlock her own seatbelt. And then he leaned over the center console, covering her overheated body with his.

She screamed when his hand covered her clit.

"That feel good?" he asked.

"That's the only dumb thing you've said to me all night," she said.

He smiled down at her, still rubbing hard circles over her clit. Then he moved his free hand behind her neck, pushed her fingers aside at her aching core and replaced them with his own in a forceful thrust that made Cleo's back arch.

"Oh fuck," she breathed, shuddering.

He started fucking her in slow, deliberate strokes with three fingers, his thumb still grazing her clit.

"Give me your other finger," she begged.

His grip tightened on her neck. "Ask me nicely," he demanded.

That made her moan so loudly she might have just yelled.

He wasn't fazed. He just kept fucking her and holding her against his chest, watching her come undone, waiting.

"Please," she gasped, circling her hips, desperately trying to get those fingers deeper inside her pussy, as deep as they could go. "Please put another finger inside me."

He lowered his head and sucked her bottom lip into his mouth, leaning back to let it slip through his teeth. How did he know she'd like the soft pain of that? she thought. But it really didn't matter, since he'd pushed that last finger into her cunt. She felt full and stretched. It was perfect.

Now that the wind wasn't howling in their ears, they could both hear the wet squelch of her pussy fighting to keep his hand inside her. It was obscene, made even more so by the way he stared down at her, holding her gaze, as if he didn't want to miss a millisecond of her pleasure. As if getting her off was serious business.

"Good girl," he whispered against her lips. "Now feed me your fingers."

"Oh god." She didn't waste a second complying.

He kept his eyes glued on her and his hand fucking her while she slipped her wet fingers into his mouth.

She watched him lick and suck her essence from her digits, his tongue swirling around each one individually. All of a sudden there was nothing else, not a heist on the horizon, not a crew she was responsible for, hell even the car disappeared. In that moment Cleo couldn't concentrate on anything but the coming orgasm and the way Mr. Shimizu felt inside and on top of her.

Her eyes slammed shut. "Oh fuck, I'm gonna come. Fuckfuckfuck."

He moved his mouth from her hand only briefly, and Cleo already knew what he would say. "Ask m—"

"Please, fuck, please let me come, Mr. Shimizu," she whined.

"Of course," he said, kissing her wet knuckle. "Come."

There are orgasms, and then there are life-changing moments between your legs. Cleo had had many of the former and a few of the latter. But this orgasm was different. It was transcendent. She felt as if she were floating above herself, somewhere up in the ether. From that vantage point, she looked down at herself; half-naked, splayed out, a complete stranger's whole hand stuffed almost entirely inside her pussy as she came in a wet gush on his Italian leather seats, and she smiled down in smug approval at her life choices. This orgasm was life affirming and earth shattering.

And through it all, Mr. Shimizu kept sawing his fingers into her, drawing out the full force of her orgasm, extending the electric aftershocks until they built and built and she was coming again. And he stayed with her. His face hovered above her, calm and relaxed, his burning, excited eyes the only sign of how much he was affected by her as she shivered and shuddered in his arms.

Eventually she had to closer her thighs with a whimper, the crash of too many orgasms making her sex overly sensitive.

It took a few seconds more for her to be able to speak. "I probably ruined your seat," she whispered up at him with a hoarse voice and a small smile on her lips.

His hand had stopped moving at her core, but he didn't abandon her. He left his fingers buried deep inside her, letting her squeeze and clench around him. And then he brushed his mouth against her cheek gently. "You let me know when you're up for ruining the back seat."

"Oh fuck," she gasped.

And came again.

THREE

CLEO HAD NEVER BLACKED out during sex before. But there's a first time for everything.

When she blinked back into consciousness, it took a few seconds for her brain to boot back up to full speed.

She shivered as the car took a turn and the rushing wind hit her bare skin. She struggled to sit up straight and jumped when the car's convertible top began to ascend from the rear. Mr. Shimizu extended his hand to latch the top to the front windshield, and then back on the gear shift. He looked... composed; casual, as if he hadn't just made her come so hard she'd lost consciousness.

"How long was I out?" she croaked and cringed at her sore throat.

He smiled but kept his eyes on the road. "Not long. I took the liberty of fixing your clothes."

She looked down at her dress, which had been pulled over her ass and down her thighs as far as it would go, which wasn't far.

"You didn't put my underwear back on," she said, rubbing her thighs together.

This time he did spare her a brief glance. "I didn't."

Cleo was certain that if her body could have mustered it, she would have come again. This man really was dangerous, and she couldn't believe how much she liked it. She turned in her seat and squinted at him in the dark car. "I've never met anyone like you before," she admitted quietly.

"Thank you."

It wasn't a compliment. Not the way he took it.

An integral part of Cleo's job was being able to quickly clock the men she met. In their fleeting encounter at the poker table and in front of the Kismet party, she'd thought she'd understood him: rich, assured, capable. But she was wrong. There was something else about him. Something she couldn't put her finger on, and she wanted to. Her brain whirred, trying to make sense of the man next to her, wanting to understand what made him tick, how he could seem so calm and intense at the same time, and why he made her feel like she'd taken a hit of some designer drug only rich playboys could afford.

And all of that was a problem. Cleo was very rarely wrong about men and if asked twelve hours ago she'd have said that she'd met at least one from all the major types and knew the most dangerous categories intimately: broke and fine, hustling and scheming, rich and petty and powerful and ruthless. But Mr. Shimizu seemed to be none of those things or maybe it was that he seemed like so many of those things all jumbled together. Cleo didn't know and it would have started to drive her crazy if she weren't terrified by her reaction to him.

As a rule, Cleo never got attached to men, not even when she wanted to. But here she was in this strange man's car, desperate to know what his dick looked like and how he took his coffee. She wasn't that type of person at all.

Before she had the opportunity to fully freak out, however, he turned briefly to her and said in a dark voice that made her shiver violently, "You came without permission."

Cleo wanted to answer, but she didn't know what to say. She was also distracted by the movement of his shoulder muscles under his shirt as he made a sharp left turn.

"No, I didn't. I asked," she said, completely shocked that this was an accusation she was defending herself against, after all the many scams she'd committed tonight alone.

"You asked for the first orgasm, but not the second," he said, watching the road.

Cleo frowned at the side of his head. "I did," she admitted.

The car slowed drastically, and Cleo turned as he pulled into a gated enclave. She spotted a guard's shed and thought she saw Mr. Shimizu nod minutely, though he didn't stop. She craned her neck to see the small enclave of luxury condominiums as they passed, driving deep into the neighborhood. The further they drove, the bigger the houses got, until up ahead of them a garage door opened next to a small mansion. It wasn't as big as the house they'd just left, but she could tell, even in the dead of night that it was worth more. Cleo took that as another sign that she'd been right about one thing at least; this man was much richer than Frank Pugh III.

He pulled his car into a circular driveway, another vintage car parked out front like a statue. She recognized the Porsche 365 Speedster immediately because she'd once concocted an elaborate con to sell one to a corrupt politician desperate to misuse some campaign finances. He'd probably been so pissed when he got the replica figurine in the mail, but by then Cleo was long gone. Robert put the car in park and turned the key in the ignition as the garage door began to descend.

When she turned to him, he was watching her as if he could see inside her most private thoughts. She felt naked under that gaze, and it was as uncomfortable as it was exciting for a brief moment before it burned away in another intense wave of lust.

"How would you like to be punished?" he asked, as if that was a normal question.

But again, she didn't know him so... maybe it was. In any case, it made her wetter than the fucking ocean, so she undid her seat belt and turned fully toward him. She licked her lips. He grunted. She reached out to stroke a single long acrylic nail down the length of his tie.

"You're in charge," she said, because it wasn't a question. It was the very disconcerting truth. A truth that should have made her slip off her heels and run away from him as fast as she could. A truth that made her feel something so deep inside her marrow that she stayed right where she was instead.

"I am. Is that okay with you?"

Cleo swallowed uncomfortably. "I'm not sure yet. But I'll tell you if I change my mind."

"You do that."

"I've got two requests," she said, squaring her shoulders.

"Anything," he whispered immediately.

She swallowed a moan and took a deep breath. "First, you can't ruin my hair. This is one of my favorite wigs."

He chuckled and nodded. "Of course."

"Thank you. And second..." Cleo took a breath, unable to believe *she* was about to say these words.

But she was. She had to. She leaned forward. He mirrored her movements, meeting her over the gear shift. "Kiss me," she breathed against his lips.

She'd never asked a man to kiss her before. She'd never had to. Usually, she had to politely recoil from men who didn't know that their entire tongues didn't need to be halfway down her throat to kiss. But she didn't think she'd have that problem with Robert. She'd met him an hour ago, but she felt certain that he would treat her lips better than that. But still, she couldn't bear to look him in the eye after she made her request, so she tilted her head down and focused on the knot of his tie.

She should have known that he wouldn't let her hide from him. Not when he'd followed her from the party. Not when he'd driven like a demon just so she could feel the wind on her skin with her heart racing. Not when he'd wanted her orgasm for himself. Not when he'd wanted her wet fingers in his mouth. Not when he wanted to be in charge, but needed to know that she was okay. Not when 'anything' sounded like a promise.

Mr. Shimizu slowly released his seatbelt. She watched as he turned his body fully toward her. She held her breath as his hands moved to her face. That first touch was gentle, and then it strengthened.

He tilted her head back. "Look at me."

She swallowed again, searching for the strength to follow his clear command, no matter how soft he'd whispered it. When their eyes met, he didn't rush. Instead, he looked at her for several silent, heated seconds. He let her reacclimate to the feeling of his hands on her skin, and the air between their mouths changed from the snap of late evening to humid intensity. When their breaths had evened out and they matched one another's inhalations and exhalations, his thumb moved to trace her bottom lip.

And then he pulled her mouth to his. Their lips crushed together, deep and forceful and punishing.

Robert kissed Cleo exactly as he'd masturbated her; patiently, thoroughly, his body in complete control of hers. His tongue pushed into her mouth and gently coaxed hers forward. His lips pressed and retreated as their tongues slid against one another. His hands moved her head just a bit to the left and their kiss deepened. The pads of his ring fingers pressed gently at her pulse, soothing her, even as his mouth made her whimper in his.

Cleo held onto his wrists with a desperate grip. She didn't want this kiss to end, but she also wanted to rip his clothes off. She wanted to climb over the center console and ride him, but she also wanted him to take her into his house and fill every hole over and over again.

When he broke away, the only thing that stopped her from whining was her pride.

His thumbs smoothed over the apples of her cheeks. "Are you ready?" he asked, his voice hoarse.

"Yeah."

"I promise I'll be gentle."

Cleo reared back. "You better fucking not."

His laughter filled the garage.

▭

EVERY NOW AND THEN, Cleo met someone on a job she wished she'd have met under any another circumstances. Sometimes it was her mark's executive assistant with a great sense of style. For brief moments she'd let herself imagine being back in Chicago and meeting up with her for brunch and tipsy shopping. Once, it was the exotic dancer across the hall in the condo she'd rented to set up an oil executive with a savior complex and a bit of an embezzling problem. One night, the oil exec had had a little too much to drink, and she'd had to enlist Brian to help her get him inside her apartment. Keisha had opened her front door just as they'd dropped their mark at Cleo's front door so she could find her keys in her purse. Keisha had paused briefly to take in the scene and then shrugged. "Lift with your knees," she'd called over her shoulder as she headed off to work.

And now there was Robert Shimizu.

She waited for him to come around the car to open her door with an offered hand. She let him hold onto her and lead her inside his home. All the while, she imagined what it would have been like if they'd met while he was in town on a business trip. If he'd thought that she was some lawyer's executive assistant or a freelance makeup artist. A part of her also wondered if she could have pretended that she was just a normal woman for a few weeks before exposing herself as the kind of person who would masturbate in a convertible going a hundred miles an hour. She wondered if under the right circumstances this could have been more than just one night.

But that was a foolish thought, just like all the other times she'd imagined that she was someone different. These people she daydreamed about folding into her life didn't know her, not really. They encountered a version of Cleo that was at best some alternate version of herself, but more like a pure fabrication. To do her job well, she had to become the person the mark wanted – whoever they needed to see – so her team could rob him blind. She wasn't the kind of woman who giggled instead of answered, who thought some drunk and belligerent trust fund kid was sexy or who let a complete stranger be in control.

Granted, she'd been as close to herself as was possible from the minute Mr. Shimizu had offered his coat. But still, Cleo wasn't this person following him into his dark house, hoping he would press her up against a wall and fuck her until she couldn't stand. Was she?

And even if she was, that didn't matter because chances were high that he wasn't being himself either. She didn't know anything about Robert Shimizu, not really. As she followed behind him, she reasoned with herself that this entire night was a fantasy. She also reminded herself not to get attached — not to want more than tonight — and not just because it was all artifice, but because if tomorrow or next month or two years from now, Frank Pugh III asked him about the woman in the bright red wig, stripper heels and lace, she didn't want Robert to be able to tell him anything more than that her name was Cleo and her pussy was the best he ever had. That would have to be enough.

He led her through the kitchen and living room and upstairs. Cleo wasn't stupid, so she made note of where the front door was. She looked into the open doors on either side of the hallway as she passed. She stayed alert and aware. She would have been stupid not to. It wasn't a full reconnaissance and Alex would lose her entire shit if she knew how reckless Cleo was being right now. But it would have to do.

When he flicked the bedroom light on, he turned to her and ushered her inside.

"Would you like a drink?" he asked.

She saw a bar in the corner of the bedroom. She'd just bet there was a big ass Jacuzzi tub in the bathroom, maybe even a steam room or whatever other spa shit was in vogue for the rich and frivolously wealthy the last time he'd had his house redecorated.

She turned around to see him leaning casually against the doorjamb. Watching her.

She wished she could say yes, because she would have loved a little Hennessy to celebrate a job well done and the sex to come. She wished she could tell him that they could take the drink downstairs and talk about sports or movies or whatever the fuck. They didn't have to rush and could ease into one another gently. She wanted to tell him that there wasn't any rush and they could work up to fucking each other's brains out. But they didn't have time for lies. And wasn't that the fucking rub. Cleo had days, weeks, months to convince other rich men to give up their computer passwords, but she didn't have time to let this rich man make good on every check his eyes and the bulge of his erection was writing.

She turned her head and spotted a clock on the wall above his dresser. In fifteen minutes, her crew would start slowly emptying Frank's house. In two hours, all the guests would be gone and they'd clean him out in the blink of an eye and then they'd scatter. And no matter how good she knew this sex was about to be, by the time the sun was up, she needed to be on her way as well. They didn't have any time to waste.

She walked toward him, loving the way his eyes felt on her bare skin. She put her hands on his chest and pressed her front to his. She moaned deep in her throat when she felt the more than impressive bulge in his pants against her core. "Unless the drink you're offering is your come down my throat, I'm good."

"Noted," was all he said, before he completely wrecked her for every other man.

One second, he was grabbing her at the waist to spin her toward the bed, and the next, he was pulling her over his lap.

"Higher," he practically barked at Cleo.

She walked on her tip toes to get her ass up in the air.

He pulled her dress over her ass. She heard a few threads rip. Normally, that would have pissed her off — this dress had not been cheap — but not right now. This time it only ratcheted up her arousal. As did his big hand gently rubbing the globes of her ass.

"Beautiful," he said as he squeezed her right cheek hard in his hand.

"Fuck," Cleo groaned.

He released her flesh. "We'll get there. Don't worry." And then his hand collided with her right cheek, the sound of flesh meeting flesh ringing in her ears.

"Is that okay?" he asked.

"Harder," she ground out.

He chuckled and grabbed her left ass cheek,

lightly smacking it; toying with her. "Who's in charge?"

She turned her head in frustration and found him smiling playfully.

"Answer me," he barked.

"You," she moaned.

"What do you say?"

She gasped before she could answer. "Please spank me harder."

He nodded once and held her gaze as he smacked her left cheek again, this time much harder.

Cleo yelped and licked her lips.

"Can you take more?" he asked.

She nodded.

He grabbed her right cheek and squeezed just shy of hard enough to hurt. He shook his head.

"Yes," she whined. "Please."

He smacked each cheek with a sharp tap of his hand back and forth, his eyes on her the entire time.

She started to squirm in his lap, but she couldn't look away either. She wanted to imprint every moment of this night on her brain; she needed to remember it all.

"If you want more," he said, rubbing her warm cheeks, soothing them, "just ask nicely."

"Oh god," she moaned. "Please, spank me some more, Mr. Shimizu."

He smiled this time as his free hand gently circled her neck in a possessive hold that was tight, but not enough to restrict her air. His hand at her throat made her feel safe and secure. She'd never felt anything like this before and she closed her eyes in pleasure, relaxing across his lap.

He held her and waited until her eyelids fluttered open again. And he kept his gaze on her as really spanked her this time, alternating between each cheek, moving between sharp taps of his fingertips that stung in the most delicious way and flat palm against bouncing flesh that made her cry out in ecstasy.

Cleo's gasps turned to groans and then moans. Her eyes were wet with unshed tears. Her thighs were slick with her arousal. Mr. Shimizu kept his eyes on her as she came undone on top of him, squirming against his erection. She' never known it could be like this. She'd never known feeling like this was even a possibility.

When he stopped, her ass was hot, tingling, and so was her pussy.

"Good girl," he whispered before brushing his mouth against her temple.

They were both breathing hard, their breaths as in tune as their sex drives.

Cleo shut her eyes. He whispered soft kisses at the edge of her wig lace and eventually the tears in her eyes finally fell down her cheeks. It was such an unexpectedly gentle moment, and even that was a new sensation. And so was the abrupt turn as Mr.

Shimizu shoved his hand between her ass cheeks, skimming her backdoor and perineum and then pushing into her soaked cunt.

"Oh fuck," Cleo screamed.

"Keep your legs tight," he ground out when she tried to spread herself wider for him.

"Fuckfuckfuck," she moaned and crossed her legs at the ankles.

She shuddered on his lap as he moved his fingers inside her in shallow thrusts; not enough to get her off, but enough to make her leak all over his hand. She tried to ride his fingers and that mound at the same time. She hoped she ruined his suit.

But all too soon, he wrenched his hand from between her legs and smacked her ass with a wet tap. Small shudders rippled through her sex and her head fell forward in shock mingling with pleasure. His hand moved from her neck to cup the side of her face almost lovingly for a second, his fingers stroking her chin.

"On your knees," he breathed. He eased her from his lap to the floor as he stood in front of her, her face level with his erection.

Cleo wiped at her eyes, mostly so that her tears didn't obscure her first look at his dick. She needed to see it in all its glory.

He placed a hand behind her neck and moved the other hand to her face, wiping at her tears briefly before letting that arm fall to his side.

Cleo's eyes were glued on his bulge. She was desperate to see it, feel it and taste it, now. But she also knew she had to wait. She wasn't normally the kind of woman who liked to wait, ever, but he made each second of quiet calm feel as if the air was buzzing with electricity. It ramped up her arousal; made her heartbeat pound in her ears and her sex clench with need.

This was more than foreplay. Cleo didn't know what this was, but she knew she liked it far more than she should. And even knowing that the desperate lust she felt was a red flag, it still made her sex weep down her inner thighs in expectant excitement.

The room was quiet but for their labored breaths and the muffled sound of the central heat kicking on. They listened to the seconds tick by on the manual clock on the wall in perfect silence. Eventually, he tightened his grip around her neck and his thumb stroked the sensitive skin just behind her right ear. He calmed her.

And then finally, after far too long, she lifted her eyes to his, and that pleased him.

"Take me out," he said in a barely restrained command.

Cleo moved her knees together and clenched. Her pride took a bit of a hit when she saw her hands shaking on his belt buckle – Calvin Klein, snakeskin, maybe vintage – but she worked through it. She tore his belt open without a care in the world of how much it cost, but she took her time unzipping his pants

He grunted and involuntarily thrust his hips forward.

She smiled up at him.

He raised an eyebrow, but he didn't say the word that was on the tip of his tongue — like she wanted the head of his dick to be on hers — so she said it for him.

"Hurry?"

He smiled but said nothing.

Cleo moved to rub his erection from outside his pants, teasing him, teasing herself, but only for a second. When she pulled his slacks down his legs, his bulge was even more impressive in the thin black Ralph Lauren boxer briefs. If they had more than just tonight Cleo would have happily spent an entire hour just admiring that dick print, but they didn't have time for all that, so she pulled his briefs down and there he was. Hard, fat, veiny, an angry red at the tip, sticking straight up toward the ceiling, beautifully manicured pubic hair, big balls hanging, amazing. Robert Shimizu's dick called to her like a pair of Cartier cufflinks on a man who wouldn't even miss them until the next day. If Cleo could have crafted her perfect dick, it would have been this one. And if she could have attached it to a man, Mr. Shimizu was turning out to be a pretty good option. But then his free hand blocked her from taking hold of him and feeling the weight of him in her palm.

"Wha—" she said, frowning up at him.

"Hands behind your back."

She shivered as she complied. She groaned when his hand wrapped around his dick. She watched as he pumped himself twice, angling the tip toward her mouth and then away.

She glared up at him, licking her lips.

His smile was bigger than ever. "Open your mouth."

Her lips fell apart at the first word.

"Would you like a drink?" he asked in that same calm, polite voice from before.

"God, yes," she panted. She thought the invitation was clear, but she didn't want to take a chance that he might misunderstand. "Use my mouth," she breathed, and then stuck her tongue out for him.

"I plan to."

He held her gaze as he moved the tip of his dick to her tongue. The first taste of him made Cleo groan. He rubbed the soft spongy head from the tip of her tongue up to her lips and then back again, smearing his precome across her taste buds.

"Taste me," he said.

She didn't need to be told twice. She closed her mouth and let his saltiness coat her mouth, before eagerly opening her mouth for more.

This time, he moved his dick up the length of her

tongue and rested its weight there for a second. And then he took a step forward and slipped the head of his dick past her lips a little bit at a time.

She whined when he pulled away and groaned when he pushed back inside. Cleo was conflicted. Each time he pushed inside of her mouth, her pussy clenched and her hips rolled at how soft and slow and gentle he was. But she also wanted more, faster, harder. When she looked up at him with the plea for him to give her what she wanted clearly evident in her eyes, she saw the mirth in his.

And then she remembered.

This time, when his hips moved back, she closed her mouth and sucked on the tip so hard, his back bowed and his body jumped. His dick came free with a vulgar pop that made them both groan.

Before he could push into her again, she spoke. "Please," she panted, "fuck my mouth, Mr. Shimizu."

His shoulders sagged in relief. "Of course," he whispered, and then pushed the tip of his dick between her lips. He moved both hands to the side of her head, being careful of her hair. She opened her mouth as wide as it would go, loving being filled with him as he pressed further inside.

When he touched the back of her throat, he stopped and let her adjust. She closed her eyes when she had, silently giving him permission to continue.

Just like the drive, he started off slow, moving in

and out of her mouth with good, steady pressure, his hips picking up speed incrementally.

"Put your hands on my thighs," he said in a strained rasp as he began to fuck her mouth in deep, sharp thrusts of his hips.

She was moaning and drooling around his dick, her cheeks hollowed around him, a puddle certainly forming on the carpet between her legs.

"Fuck," he rasped, until it was a chant accentuating each press forward and retreat.

Cleo opened her eyes but she couldn't see anything; her vision was completely obscured by tears. The blurry vision of this ridiculously calm man falling apart above her, inside her, made her feel powerful in ways an elaborate heist never had. Cleo dug her nails into the back of his thighs, encouraging him to fuck her harder.

Soon enough he was jackhammering into her mouth bent nearly in half. The faster he fucked her, the more she drooled around his dick and onto her breasts, which only encouraged her to fuck her mouth more insistently. Eventually, his strokes began to falter and his body was wracked with spasms. Cleo's nails were digging into the back of his legs and her tongue was massaging the underside of his dick until finally he emptied inside her waiting mouth. She swallowed him deeper as he came, gulping his release down her throat greedily.

"Fuck, Cleo," he hissed. "Fuck."

When his dick stopped twitching, she pushed at his thighs. He took two shaky steps backward and his dick fell from her mouth. She looked up at where she thought his face was, her mouth open so he could see the reservoir of the last of his come inside her mouth, and then she pressed her lips shut and swallowed every drop.

"Fuckfuckfuck, Cleo," he said, pulling her to her feet and throwing her onto the bed.

When Cleo giggled this time, it was real.

FOUR

ROBERT SHIMIZU HAD NEVER BEEN PARTICULARLY interested in casual sex, but he wasn't necessarily a relationship man either. He often went months — sometimes upwards of a year — without sex, and he never thought twice about it. When his physical urges reached a breaking point, he had no problem finding someone to help him sate his appetites; a single night working off all that pent-up sexual energy was enough for him to reset his focus and get back to work. And the minute he'd seen Cleo slide her perfectly rounded hip on the arm of Frank Pugh's chair, he'd known that she was the woman he wanted to help him break his current spell of celibacy and he'd immediately begun working on how to get her off of Frank's chair and into his lap.

What he hadn't been able to guess was how absolutely perfect her body would feel against his skin.

How addicting her fingers would taste in his mouth, covered in her the taste of her pussy. And he certainly hadn't been prepared for that persistent niggling thought in the back of his head, whispering softly that one night wouldn't be enough.

And now, seeing her face down, ass up on his bed was overwhelming in its rightness and it made his dick twitch between his legs, trying to rally far too soon after shooting a bucket of come down her throat. It wasn't happening, but he knew just how to buy himself time. He pushed her knees apart and then practically shoved his face between her legs, licking her essence from her inner thighs, cleaning up every drop of her arousal. He flattened his tongue against her skin, making sure he didn't miss a drop of her.

When he was certain that he'd cleaned her up well, he moved his hands to the globes of her ass, still slightly warm from his earlier spanking. He used his thumbs to pull the lips of her cunt open. His mouth practically watered at the thought of tasting her at the source. Her wet lips clung together, enticing him, but he forced himself to wait so he could admire every inch of her. Robert wanted to sear the look and taste and smell of Just Cleo into his brain. He wanted to be able to call her to mind, in a month or in five years, and sink back into the memory of this moment. He wanted to remember her and he'd never had that feeling before.

The shocking bright pink of her pussy hiding between her brown lips called to him and finally he was too overcome to ignore it. When he flattened his tongue against her opening, she practically bucked back against his face. She tasted as perfect as she had in the car, maybe even better after so many orgasms. That intrusive thought emerged again, louder this time, chanting that this wouldn't be enough; he might never get enough. He ignored it as best he could, but he also a silent promise as his tongue pushed into her, that there was so much more to come.

She screamed filthy curses, muffled by his sheets, groaning about how desperate she was to finally feel his dick inside her. To stop fucking with her. To fuck with her some more. To fuck her now. She screamed louder and louder and Robert loved it. He wanted more.

When she came on his tongue, he felt... Robert felt. He'd never been stingy about making sure that his partners were satisfied – he fed off of their energy as much as his own – but there was something different about Cleo. Each time she came, Robert didn't feel satisfaction, he felt a deep hunger for more — more of her moans and shivering body and shaking thighs, that burrowed deeper into his gut. This was a completely brand new sensation and he didn't know what to do with it.

But he did know what to do with the arousal

leaking from her clenching sex. He licked her clean and she shuddered around another orgasm before slouching onto the bed with a tired whimper.

"Condoms," she groaned, sounding as exhausted as he felt excited. "Please."

He clapped her ass with both hands, the sound of their skin smacking together like a jolt of electricity to his spend dick. He stood from the bed and watched her as he pulled his pants and underwear from his ankles. He walked to the bathroom and stole peeks of her over his shoulder, not wanting to miss a second of drinking her in. He found the brand new box of condoms under the sink and hurried back into the bedroom. He stopped by the side of the bed just to look at her, marveling at her beautiful face pressed into the comforter, certainly smearing it with her makeup and tears, and her big round ass back in the air, waiting for him.

He threw the box of condoms next to her on the bed. He didn't miss the small whimper that fell from her lips. He watched her as he carefully tugged his tie from around his neck and unbuttoned his shirt. His dick had mercifully come back to life.

Her hips began to circle in the air. He smiled at how beautiful desperation looked on her. He knew her sex must have been clenching, begging for him, and he didn't have the self-control to make her — or himself — wait any longer.

He considered stripping her dress from her body

so he could see every inch of her, but he reconsidered, unwilling to move her from this position just yet. Besides, the first thing he'd thought when he laid eyes on Cleo was that she was the kind of perfectly manicured exterior that he would enjoy deconstructing piece by piece, and he'd been right. Watching her fall apart for him in his car and now in his bedroom had been wonderful and seeing her disheveled and messy on his bed was even better.

"Fuck me," she demanded.

"Tsk tsk tsk," he said, picking the box of condoms up and ripping it open.

He slowly rolled a condom down his shaft and watched as she fisted the covers beneath her.

"Please fuck me, Mr. Shimizu," she whined.

"You keep forgetting to ask me to come," he said as he walked to the foot of the bed.

She whimpered some more as the mattress dipped and he settled behind her, pushing her knees further apart with his own. "I won't forget this time," she hissed, when the front of his thighs met the back of hers.

He stroked his dick as he watched her squirm beneath him. "We'll see," he whispered and then pushed into her in one long, deep thrust.

Technically, this was bad timing. Robert really couldn't afford to spend the entire night fucking Cleo; he had a full day of work tomorrow. He needed to meet with his second-in-command, go over some contracts, review the background checks of his new hires. He had a busy life that required he be well-rested and alert, that's why he usually planned his sexual encounters very carefully. Meeting Cleo was going to fuck up his schedule and he didn't care. The minute he felt Cleo's wet heat surround his aching cock, nothing that would come tomorrow was more important than staying right where he was. He had no plans to spend any more time sleeping tonight than was absolutely necessary and he'd just have to deal with the consequences because they would be worth it; Cleo was worth it.

He pulled out of Cleo's pussy to the tip and she desperately pushed back onto him. He smiled and pressed his hips forward, as needy to be inside of her as she was to have him there. Her muffled cries became hoarse and ragged and hysterical. His pulse was pounding in his ears like a stampede. It was perfect and then even better when she kept her word and cried out to him.

"Please can I come, Mr. Shimizu? Pleasepleaseplease," she screamed.

How could he tell her no?

"Come," he ground out through clenched teeth. And fuck if she didn't feel amazing as he fucked her through that spasming orgasm.

And then she asked again and again, each time she was close.

He barked at her to come and then fucked her

hard, rewarded with her clenching pussy shuddering around his dick, milking him. The said yes as his back bowed, his muscles strained and began to hurt, his hair became limp with sweat, because he didn't want to tell her now and he never wanted this night to end. Robert wasn't a man interested in casual sex or relationships, but there was nothing casual about the way Cleo felt coming on his dick and if relationships were like this, maybe he needed to rethink his stance.

It had been half a year since he'd had sex, and if Cleo was who he'd been waiting for, she was worth it. It hadn't ever been nearly as good as this with anyone else, and Robert wanted to savor it and her.

And he did.

The hours melted away as they used almost the entire box of condoms. He rode Cleo and then she returned the favor. They ruined the sheets with her makeup and come and sweat. They ruined each other, Robert thought. But he knew for certain that Cleo had ruined him for anyone else. They fucked and sucked until they had literally nothing left to give.

They were out of breath, their throats were stripped, and their muscles were aching. They were too tired to even spoon and just passed out next to one another as the sun was beginning to lighten the sky. It was hands down, the best night of Robert's life.

CLEO WOKE UP WITH A START.

She would have admonished herself for falling asleep in a stranger's house when she needed to get to running, but she'd never been fucked into a deep sleep before, so she gave herself a bit of grace as she blinked back into consciousness. Her throat was raw and aching and so was her pussy. She felt wrecked but energized.

She slipped out of Robert Shimizu's bed but didn't run away immediately, even though she definitely should have. She stood next to the bed and looked down at him, taking in his naked unguarded body in the early morning light. Besides the fact that her pussy was actually throbbing from overuse and she was worried she might not be able to lift her arms over her head because her muscles were so weak, she wanted to crawl back into his bed and climb on top of him again and that was a shocking thought. Even scarier was that she really wanted to curl into his side and feel his lean body against hers, listen to his deep breathing and soft snores rumble in his chest until he woke up naturally next to her.

But nah, she absolutely couldn't do either of those things, so she forced herself to turn away. She tiptoed around the bedroom, locating her dress, purse and shoes all scattered on the carpeted floor, not entirely sure when she'd even taken any of those things off.

She cringed as she stepped into her dress. It was covered in her makeup and his come; filthy. Or maybe it was her come? Someone's come. This was why she'd never been the stay the night one-night stand kind of woman, the morning after was a mess. But it had been worth it, she thought with a shrug, so she made do. When her good bits were mostly covered, she grabbed her purse in one hand, her shoes in the other and walked as quietly as she could from the room.

She made it as far as the door before the full scale of the previous night hit her; the good, the great and the confusing and her body tried to revolt, because she wanted to stay. But she forced herself to focus and deal with the most pressing matter at hand: she'd left her car at Frank's house. It didn't really matter since it was stolen, but how was she going to get out of here? She only had to wonder at that briefly, because the answer was very obvious.

She tiptoed back into the bedroom and plucked Robert's car keys from the crumpled heap of his pants on the floor. Her fingers touched something soft buried deep inside his pocket and she pulled on it. She held her lacy thong in her hand. She knew she should take it with her; good lingerie wasn't cheap. But a wave of unfamiliar sentimentality washed over her and she pushed her thong back inside his pants pocket. Last night had been unexpected and amazing and she wanted to leave him something to remember her by.

Especially since she was about to steal his car.

And since she was already stealing, she decided she wanted something to remember him by — when her aching body stopped throbbing — so she made her way back to the bed. She waited quietly next to Robert's prone body, listening to his melodic breathing, making sure he was really asleep. When she was certain, she quickly unsnapped his watch, kissed him on his forehead and high-tailed it from the bedroom, softly closing the door behind her.

On the way back to the garage, she grabbed a crystal ashtray she'd use to appease Alex and a banana from the fruit basket on the kitchen table. She unlocked the car, threw her loot, shoes and purse into the passenger seat and put the key in the ignition. Before she made her escape, she flipped down the visor and immediately wished she hadn't.

"Damn, girl," she breathed disapprovingly at her reflection. Her makeup was gone — fucked and sweated away — besides black raccoon smudges of mascara around her eyes. Her wig was also a shambles, but to be fair, not because of Robert alone. There was no way to have sex like they had and not ruin a wig. The lace was lifting at her edges and she wasn't even sure she'd be able to comb out the many knots. She closed the visor and sighed.

"Worth it," she said to herself and rallied. She pressed the garage door opener above the rearview mirror and turned the key in the ignition. She carefully backed out of the driveway and into the street. Her eyes kept darting to the rearview mirror, expecting — maybe even hoping — to see Robert running after her, preferably stark naked.

But it never happened.

When she made it unmolested past the security shed and out of Robert's neighborhood, she revved the engine — which made her think of Robert's grunts — and headed straight to the freeway. At a red light, she fished her phone from her purse. She sighed at all the missed calls and text messages but ignored them. She hit speed dial number one.

"Where the fuck have you been?" Alex yelled into her ear as soon as she picked up.

"A bit of a detour. Couldn't be avoided. How'd it go?"

Alex sighed in frustration. Cleo knew she wouldn't let that vague answer slide, but there was business to attend to, however many hours late. "Cleaned him out without a hitch. Everyone's on the move *except* you."

"How do you know?"

"Because I had Brian track your phone."

"Have him track me again, I'm moving."

"You missed your flight," Alex shrieked.

"Yeah, sorry about that. New plan. I'm driving to my next stop."

"What? Why? How? You left your car at the mark's house. Luckily we snatched it and dumped it for you."

Cleo smiled. "This is why you're my perfect number two. And I'll fill you in whenever I get to where I'm going, okay?"

"Fine," Alex ground out. "But you better have a damn good reason for disappearing on me."

Cleo hung up without answering her sister. She thought about telling her about last night. About Robert. She could ask Alex to discreetly investigate him, and knowing her sister, she would. But if she did that, Alex would want to rob him, or even worse, know how she felt about him. The thought made something in Cleo's stomach rumble uncomfortably at the thought of stealing from Robert — well, any more than she already had — or thinking about feelings she couldn't explain. So, she kept her mouth shut and her foot on the ignition.

There was a knot in her throat when she threw her phone back into the passenger seat. The sun was painfully bright, and she flipped open the center console where she found a pair of vintage aviator Ray-Ban sunglasses and slipped them onto her face. She bet they looked fucking perfect on Mr. Shimizu, and as it happened, they looked amazing on her as well. They didn't hide her lifting wig, but they hid her raccoon eyes, and something was better than nothing.

She pressed her left foot onto the clutch, moved the gear shift smoothly into second gear, and gunned the gas. She'd had much worse escapes from a job than driving off into the early morning sunshine in a vintage roadster, well-fucked and only a little bit remorseful.

DECEMBER

FIVE

"WHAT DO YOU THINK? Blonde? Honey blonde? Or should I give a few people a heart attack with this new pastel pink?"

"I don't care what hair you wear," Alex said.

Cleo turned from the coffee table where she'd laid out her wig choices and frowned at her sister, currently boring an angry hole in the side of her head with her gaze. "The fuck is up your ass today?"

Alex sighed and looked up at her. "You shouldn't do this job."

"Not this again." Cleo shook her head and crossed her arms over her chest.

Alex rushed around the table. "Cleo, listen to me."

"I *have* listened to you."

"Then listen *again*," Alex yelled.

Cleo sighed and shrugged with a nod.

"After the Pugh job, you said we were straight for the rest of the year."

"We are—"

"Shut up. You said you wanted to spend New Year's Eve on some tropical beach below the equator in the sunshine, drinking something strong and colorful. But here we are in Miami fucking Florida. Why?"

Cleo cut her eyes at her sister. "Oh, can I talk now?"

Alex rolled her eyes.

"You know why we're here," Cleo said. "How often do a bunch of rich ass people get together to blow too much money?"

Alex scoffed, "Every other week."

"Not like this," Cleo said.

"Bullshit. You talk about this job like it's the fucking Holy Grail. These rich motherfuckers don't have jobs, Cleo. That's what you always told me. They're rich and we need to relieve them of a little bit of that dough."

"And that's what we're doing," Cleo snapped back.

"You also told me not to be stupid. And this hasty ass plan is stupid. But if we wait and plan — like we *always* do — we can catch most of these dummies in Monte Carlo or Tokyo in a few months. So why the rush?"

"Why not? Why wait a few months when we

can clean a few of them out now and spend the winter in Switzerland skiing?"

"Bitch, you don't ski."

"I like looking at snow and wearing cute winter outfits, though."

"Something's up," Alex said suspiciously, narrowing her eyes at Cleo.

Cleo sucked her teeth and turned her back to her sister. She looked down at her wig choices, but she wasn't really seeing them. In their place was Robert Shimizu; opening his car door for her, ushering her politely inside, driving in the dark night, his hair flowing in the wind, his dark eyes watching her calmly as he fucked her with his fingers.

She could feel her body heating just thinking about those few snatches of their night together, and she couldn't let Alex see her like that. She'd spent the past six months having to hide herself from the person who knew her best, terrified that her little sister would see that the hasty one-night stand she'd told her about — "a bitch has needs" — had been more. So much more that she hadn't been able to stop thinking about it. About him. The memories kept her and her vibrator up all night. She couldn't tell Alex that because she knew she'd never understand.

But hiding the deep well of yearning was making her restless; reckless, when she'd never been. And even if Alex didn't know why, she definitely knew something was going on.

"Cleo, what the fuck?" Alex asked in a terrified whisper.

She had to take a deep breath and really work to put a smile on her face before she turned back around. "Look, I just... What if we didn't have to work so much?"

Alex reared back and pursed her lips. "We don't *have* to work this much, but we got mortgages on luxury apartments and daddy to take care of. What 9-to-5 is going to cover that? And who the fuck is going to do it? Besides," Alex continued, her face full of disgust, "if you think there ain't some law enforcement agency just waiting for us to get complacent or settle down or get *sloppy,* then I know something is really up."

"I didn't say *stop* working," Cleo corrected, even though she'd given it a fleeting thought more than once over the past six months. "I just meant work less."

"Fine. We work less. Starting now. Let's get out of here." Alex walked quickly back to the dining room table in the middle of their hotel room and slammed her laptop shut.

"No," Cleo said. "This last job, and then we slow down."

"Why?" Alex yelled at the top of her lungs.

"Because this isn't just the two of us anymore.

Brian, Marcus and Gina get a say on the jobs we take on too. And they all agreed that this opportunity is too good to pass up." As she spoke — mentally grasping at straws — her nerves settled and her voice strengthened. She hid all of her anxieties and that insatiable need for *more* behind their group dynamics to deflect her sister. It was terrible, but it worked. She could see it on Alex's frustrated face. When she spoke again, she softened her voice. "Look, if you don't want to do the job, don't. You can leave. Go home and spend New Year's Eve with daddy. Y'all can watch The Wiz and drink too much Crown and probably pass out before the ball even drops."

Alex sucked her teeth and rolled her eyes. "Please, if I go home without you, the first thing daddy gone say is, 'Where's your sister? Y'all supposed to stick together.' I'm not tryna deal with that guilt trip going into the new year, just 'cause you hardheaded."

"Then go to Rio. Or Lagos. Wherever."

"No, because I wouldn't be able to enjoy myself. Everybody around me would be having a good old drunk time and I'd be sitting in some corner tipsy, thinking about your dumb ass getting arrested wearing a tacky pink wig in your booking photo."

"Tacky?"

"Cleo!"

"Alex!"

They hadn't yelled at each other like this since Alex was a teenager stealing Cleo's B2K CDs and refusing to return them. They glared at one another across the room, chests heaving and fists clenched.

If she were anyone else on her team, Cleo would have kicked her out of her room, and maybe even off the squad. But Alex wasn't just another con artist she worked with; she was her little sister, and the only person she trusted implicitly. At the end of the day, no matter their reservations or the secrets they kept, they were in this together. It had always been just the two of them.

"Look, I know it's your job to worry about all the shit that could go wrong, but this is what we do and we're fucking great at it. But I'm getting older."

"You're twenty-eight, chill."

"I'm twenty-eight and I want to buy a house, maybe go to college or have a kid."

"With who?" Alex asked incredulously.

Cleo rolled her eyes and smiled. "I said maybe. Hell, maybe I want to meet a nice dude with a retirement plan or some shit. The point is this job will give me a little break from all the traveling to just... think about what comes next for me."

Alex's face fell.

"We can't do this forever," Cleo said.

"Why not? This is what we're good at."

"But maybe it's not the only thing we're good at. Who knows? The point is I want to find out. So we do this last job, stack our money and just be free for a year. No more boosting cars for our covers. No more aliases. No more counterfeits or fake passports or lobster-looking ass white men trying to act out some antebellum fantasy on us. We can just be regular ass people for an entire year."

Alex had never been good at hiding her emotions unless there was money on the line, and the look of pure disgust on her face was priceless. It also broke Cleo's heart.

"Why the fuck would we ever want to be regular?"

Cleo's smile was slow to come but when it did, it was like her laughter burst from her mouth. It took a second, but eventually Alex joined her. Their laughter filled the room and eased the tension between them; some of it, at least.

Cleo wiped a tear from the corner of her right eye and gave Alex the same small smile she used to when she wanted to apologize without having to actually say the words "I'm sorry."

"I don't get it," Alex said. "And I still think something's up, but I go where you go."

Cleo walked across the room and pulled Alex into a hug. "Where I go, you go," she echoed.

"If you get me locked up, I'm gonna convince my prison girlfriend to put a hit on you."

"That's fair."

———

THE GRAND PALACE Miami wasn't the fanciest hotel in the city. Not by a long shot. But it was famous. The hotel owners announced the building in 1932. It should have taken a year from ground-breaking to opening, but the mob had infiltrated all of the city's construction unions. When it finally opened in 1935, it had cost nearly three times its budget, but the biggest mobsters thought of it as *their* hangout; the center of their gambling rackets before Havana and Las Vegas pulled their clientele away. It was a fascinating history, and Cleo had been obsessed with it ever since she'd heard the whispers about the charity gala — or whatever rich name the organizers had given this poor excuse for rich people to gamble in a city where it was illegal.

She stepped into the hotel lobby, her head tilting back so she could see the mirrored ceiling. When it was first erected, the lobby ceiling had been a condensed replica of the Sistine Chapel, but now it was covered in mirrors etched lightly with the outline of the original artwork. The *Architectural Digest* article she'd read said you had to look close to see it, but it was there. If she were here on her own time, she'd have stood still and squinted until she could decipher every inch of it, but she had a job to do and there wasn't any time to waste.

At the bank of elevators, Cleo pressed the call

button and then looked at herself in the shiny gilded doors. She looked perfect, if she said so herself. Her pink wig was curled in a Marilyn Monroe style and skimmed just past her shoulders. Her makeup was so light most dumb men would assume she wasn't wearing any... even with the winged eyeliner and the glossy lipstick. But her dress was the showstopper. The structured, black off-the-shoulder cocktail dress stopped mid-thigh and hugged her close. Not that she planned to stay long enough to eat, but she'd be nervous to consume more than a single cracker in this dress, it was so tight. She turned a bit to the right and looked at her body in profile with a smile. She might not be able to breathe too deeply, but her ass was sitting high and ripe in this dress, and that was worth the momentary discomfort.

If her father had been here, he'd have said she looked like a stack of new money. That's how he'd always described her mom when they went out on date nights. And as it happened, there wasn't anything Cleo liked as much as a stack of crisp one hundred dollar bills. So yeah, she looked like brand new money, pastel pink wig and all.

When the elevator doors slid open, she stood still as the people on it stepped around her to exit and then stepped inside. She pressed the button for the twenty-fifth floor and looked out at the lobby, her eyes lifted to the ceiling one more time.

"Hold the elevator please," a man in an off-the-rack suit said, jogging toward her.

Cleo frowned and pressed the button to close the elevator door. "Sorry," she said, even though she wasn't.

She used the short ride to compose herself, something that was harder to do these days. What had once felt like putting on a second skin now felt... different. She couldn't pinpoint the exact changes, but for the past six months Cleo had been happy to shy away from buttering up some random multi-millionaire. The idea of dealing with some random man's mouth and hands on her made her want to heave. She used to be able to shirk off the attention with a graceful ease and an internal reminder that there was money to be liberated at the end of it all. But that was before she'd spent six months in near-constant arousal; her skin sensitive, tingling and needy, but only for a single set of hands.

"No," she muttered to herself. She couldn't think of Robert. Not now.

"No what?" Brian asked in his bored, robotic voice.

"Nothing," Cleo said. She took a deep breath and bounced her shoulders up and down, forcing her body to relax.

"You good?" Marcus asked. Cleo heard the sounds of a busy kitchen behind his voice.

"I'm fine," she said, just as the elevator came to a sharp stop.

Cleo took another deep breath as the doors opened. As soon as her platform patent leather heels clicked on the marble foyer, she felt fine. She felt like herself again.

She knew what to expect. Marcus and Gina had done their reconnaissance as part of the waitstaff. The twenty-fifth floor was the mezzanine area. The charity gala's organizers had turned it into a replica of the casinos in the Bellagio in Vegas, but classier. Cleo nodded in silent approval. To her left was a coat check. On her right was a bar and tight clusters of couches and chairs with people lounging across them.

She could have rolled her eyes. You've been to one rich white gala, you'd been to them all. Men were scattered around the room in expensive but slightly disheveled clothes, with much younger female escorts hanging off their arms; pristine, quiet, bored, boring. Interspersed in the crowd were a few boring queer couples with near-similar dynamics. It was all so...uninspiring.

Cleo didn't like to judge, but being some rich asshole's arm candy wasn't her bag and never would be, and not just because she was a bit prone to lifting their expensive watches. Cleo had never wanted to be a rich man's possession, however temporary. She'd thought that being in the con game made her different, but to some degree she still had to play into that role. She had to pretend that money gave these people the right to treat people like capital and she hated it. For years it had fueled her desire to rob them blind, but somewhere along the way, she'd lost the desire for even that. She wanted more, different. She didn't know what that might look like yet, but she did know that she couldn't do this for much longer. And she used that realization to stiffen her spine as she walked straight down the foyer from the elevator toward a small table for registration.

There were two pretty, basically identical white girls sitting there; one blonde, one redhead.

"How may we help you?" the redhead asked with a wide smile. The other woman's eyes flitted to take in Cleo's outfit before moving dismissively away.

"I'm here to register for the poker game," Cleo said.

The blonde cut in. "That game is invitation only."

"Invitation or a $100,000 buy-in," Cleo corrected.

"That's right," the cheery redhead said, as if Cleo was dumb. "Will you be buying in?" she asked skeptically.

Cleo was ready to tell her that yes, she would. She wanted to look these two smug bitches in the face and tell them that not only was she going to buy into this game, she was going to clean everyone in this room out and when she left, she'd be taking the pens they were using just to be petty. She'd let them keep their cheap jewelry though, she thought to herself. But that wouldn't serve her plans so she took a deep breath to calm her nerves.

She let her brain compose a string of scathing responses she knew she couldn't say, and never got the chance to anyway. Because when she opened her mouth, someone cut her off.

"I'm covering her buy-in."

It was one night. Just a few hours, really. Six months ago.

Cleo had spent ten times as long with other men and quickly forgotten their names once they were out of sight. But she'd never forgotten that voice. In fact, the past six months had only made the memory of it that much clearer, sharper. That deep but soft burr crawled under her clothing again, stroking the points of her nipples and the hair on her mound like his hands and mouth once had. That voice felt like danger and fun and coming home, all at once.

She turned slowly, hoping she was wrong, praying she wasn't.

It had only been six months, but the man in front of her looked different and completely the same. Cleo couldn't help but catalogue each difference; his hair was an inch or two longer but neater now, his beard was thicker and shot through with gray. But it was all the things that hadn't changed that preoccupied her mind. His eyes were still dark and intense, his mouth still soft and playful. And when he reached out to grab her left wrist, she swallowed hard, because his grip was still firm enough to make her want to moan.

"Cleo, what's up?" Marcus asked.

She didn't answer.

Instead, she focused on trying to keep her body in check as Robert pulled her to him, his other hand grabbing onto her waist in an iron grip.

"It's nice to see you again, Just Cleo. How do you want to be punished?" he whispered into her ear.

SIX

ROBERT SHIMIZU WASN'T a patient man, even though sometimes people assumed that he was. They often mistook his control for calm, but those were not the same things at all. Personally and professionally, he didn't want things hastily thrown together; he wanted the best. He wanted exactly what he wanted. To that end, he could accept that some things took longer than he would like to come to fruition. That didn't mean that he would wait forever, just that he was willing to wait a while to get everything he knew he deserved; the best.

But waiting six months to see Cleo Wright in the flesh again was too long.

Six months ago he'd woken up in his home, his balls aching, his throat so dry his voice cracked, and his stomach growling. But most importantly, he was alone. After he'd passed out with Cleo in a heap next to him, his unconscious brain had conjured a series of vivid scenarios he couldn't wait to realize with her over the next days, weeks, years. He'd woken up tired and sore and hard, more than ready for her again only to find his bed and garage empty.

He'd known before he'd even stumbled out of the bedroom that his car would be gone, but he hadn't realized until he'd downed half a glass of water that his father's watch was missing as well. Losing that family heirloom had stung. It was the only thing he had left of the man. He'd grown so accustomed to its weight on his wrist that he felt off balance without it. Robert felt a bright flash of anger at his bare wrist, but it was fleeting. As angry as he felt, what undercut it all was a kind of despondency he wasn't used to. He showered and changed, walking back into his bedroom in a fresh suit, clipping a new watch onto his wrist.

He'd looked at his wrecked bedsheets, covered in smudges of her brown makeup, and finally understood what he was feeling. The watch was irreplaceable, but his memories of his father and the family photo albums, which Cleo hadn't touched, were more important. The car was insured and nothing but a flashy toy, really. But to his core, the thing Robert had been most angry about Cleo taking — the thing that surprisingly mattered most — was herself.

Robert owned the best private security firm in four states and growing. He had expertly trained crews in Kentucky, Virginia, Tennessee and Indiana. Normally, he didn't go on jobs, but he'd gone to Harvard with the owner of Kismet Diamonds, so he'd tagged along as an extra set of eyes for a job no one expected to be dangerous in the least. He hadn't expected any problems, and technically there weren't any. But when he finally found his cellphone in his suit pants from the night before, he saw that he had half a dozen missed calls from his head of security and a text message telling him that Frank Pugh had been robbed after they left.

"What should we do, boss?" his number two, Stevie, had asked.

"Do?" Robert asked, shocked, his eyes still trained on his bed.

"Yeah. About the crew that cleaned that guy's place out."

Robert's first thought was an image of Frank Pugh's greedy eyes on Cleo's bare thighs and cleavage. He'd wanted to tell Stevie that it sucked he'd been robbed, but maybe he should spring for his own home security system. He'd wanted to tell Stevie that their contract was with Kismet, not Frank Pugh, so there was nothing for them *to* do. He'd wanted to scoff and tell Stevie that it sucked that bastard got robbed, but he didn't actually care.

But then his mind had pulled forward a picture of Cleo's face. Her eyes were big and sad, her lush mouth had drifted into a frown. He'd asked her if she wanted a drink and wherever her brain had gone, she looked... regretful, hurried, sad. And he knew in that moment that whoever the hell Just Cleo was, she was connected to Frank Pugh's robbery.

"Get me a copy of the police report as soon as it's in the system," Robert had said, heading back downstairs. He'd grabbed the keys to the Porsche and headed out the front door. "And ask Detective Flores if he can put a discreet BOLO out on my Jag."

"Your car got stolen?" Stevie asked.

Robert's hand had stuttered toward the ignition and stopped. He took a deep breath, contemplating all his options. "No," he finally said. "I'm letting a friend borrow it. But I need it back."

He'd almost said "her."

IT TOOK him nearly four months to figure out that Just Cleo was Cleo Wright. He burned through every contact he had, on the wrong and right sides of the law, investigating crimes that seemed eerily similar to Frank Pugh's casual home invasion. Along the way, he'd been frustrated, angered, and eventually even a little bit impressed at Cleo's gang's reputation and her impressive collection of wigs.

There was an international notice for a group of indeterminate composition wanted in the EU for a string of art heists; a woman with long bone-straight black hair was suspected of colluding with them. In Argentina, a group "of some size" was suspected of swindling nearly three million dollars from a famed winemaker in a counterfeit land deal, and the winemaker suggested that a Black American woman with honey blonde hair "and a large beautiful posterior" might be involved, although he stressed that he would not like her to be arrested. The unofficial word on that case was that the winemaker would like to marry the woman who might — "or might not, he keeps saying" — have been involved in the theft. Domestically, there were too many crimes for him to even wrap his head around. A car theft ring in Las Vegas that was maybe connected to robberies of vacation homes in Lake Tahoe, that may or may not have grown out of some fake Airbnb rentals in the area but were definitely connected to a cross-country black market in identity theft. It was staggering. Impressive. Terrible.

And none of it made Robert any less obsessed with finding her again.

He spent months digging through grainy surveillance images from all over the world, focusing on the blurry images of the woman suspected of being involved in a string of robberies targeting rich, horny men, too embarrassed to fully disclose their relationship with her or reluctant to tie a woman they hoped to get back with federal crimes. Besides, few people were certain it was the same woman in all of these cases, and Robert could understand that. The image quality was so low-grade and the woman's hair seemed to change constantly, so Robert could understand why there was such confusion on the part of people who'd never met her. But Robert recognized Cleo immediately. He didn't focus on her ever-changing hair or even bother trying to decipher facial features in such bad images. Instead, his gaze traversed the contours of her body. He would know her hips anywhere; he'd dug his fingers into them so hard while she rode him that he'd probably left marks. He'd traced every inch of her soft thighs with his hands and his mouth. And he'd spent every day since she'd disappeared with his father's watch and his favorite convertible reliving every second they'd spent together.

Robert Shimizu would have recognized Cleo Wright anywhere.

But figuring out who she was, was only half the battle. Once he knew, he had to find her, and that proved none too easy.

In the meantime, Robert had been forced to use those security images to... slake his thirst. He hadn't planned to download them a month after she'd disappeared. Or pull them up that night as he walked naked around his bedroom "to get a bit of work done before bed," the same bed where she'd fucked him to sleep. By the time he was pouring lube on the head of his dick, however, planning didn't matter; all he could feel was lust as he jacked himself off to those blurry images of the con artist he was methodically – albeit desperately – searching for.

It was during one of those... sessions... that he realized the best way to find Cleo was to make her come to him.

Somewhere in the back of his mind — probably the same place where he'd buried that persistent voice that said he didn't just want to find Cleo, he *had* to — he'd hoped she might show up at his doorstep. She hadn't. And she probably never would. And then his plan was clear. All he had to do was lay out some bait and set a trap. And what better trap for a woman who liked to relieve rich men of their money and prized possessions? A charity gambling tournament.

A scammer's buffet.

SEVEN

CLEO TOOK a step back for each step Robert Shimizu took toward her — although not a big one.

When the back of her legs hit the registration table, she took a deep breath, and he took hold of her right forearm. His grip was firm, but not too tight. To an onlooker, it probably looked casual, but there was nothing casual about the flips Cleo's stomach was doing, or the hard flint in his eyes. She couldn't tell if he was going to hand her over to the police or bend her over the table and fuck her for everyone to see. She shouldn't have, but she shivered at the uncertainty of it all. In response, his other hand gripped her waist, much too hard to be casual, and pulled her body flush with his.

Robert's head dipped forward. Her lips fell open as his mouth came closer and closer to hers.

"Did you miss me?" he asked.

Her soft gasp was the only answer she could offer, and it was so inappropriate. She should have been terrified, but she was thrilled, her pussy especially. She should have been trying to figure out how to get out of his grip, this hotel, this state asap, but all she could think about was what his thick beard — a new addition — would feel like rubbing across the hard points of her nipples. She tilted her chin up, not enough to brush their mouths together; not yet.

His fingers dug into her thick waist and she was certain she felt a hard protrusion between them.

"Did you miss me?" he whispered again.

She licked her lips, the tip of her tongue just brushing his mouth. "Depends. You here to arrest me or get on your knees?"

His hands involuntarily clenched around her, obliterating any confusion about whether or not he was hard. She imagined slipping her hand between them, unzipping his pants and stroking his dick right here, right now, in the middle of this crowded event. In fact, Cleo had spent six months dreaming of all the things she wanted to do to Mr. Shimizu if she ever saw him again.

"I'm not a cop," he said. "But I can get some handcuffs if that'll get you wet."

"I've got an entire drawer full of handcuffs. And I'm already wet. So if you're not here to arrest me..."

"Just because I'm not a cop doesn't mean I'm just going to let an international con artist go."

Cleo melted into his hold and smiled up at him, flashing her long, false eyelashes seductively at him. She put her hands on his broad chest. His perfectly tailored suit felt butter soft and expensive.

"You think I'm an artist?" she asked in the kind of come hither purr most men loved.

"I think your body is art, and I think anyone who can steal as much money from as many men as you have, isn't stupid and definitely shouldn't be trusted."

"If you're trying to distract me with compliments while you wait for the cops to show, it's working. Compliments make me horny," she admitted.

"So do fast cars," he said. The right side of his mouth tilted up into an almost smile and his head dipped just a fraction of a fraction of an inch closer to hers.

She licked her lips again. Licked his lips.

"What if I told you I wasn't going to turn you in?"

"I'd remind you that you just said I'm not stupid. Try again. Or just ask me to fuck you one more time before you let me go. That's what you want, isn't it?"

He smirked and jutted his hips forward to rub his erection against her thigh. "What is it that you want?"

"You seem to have done your homework. You can answer your own question, don't you think?"

"Tsk tsk tsk," he said softly.

Cleo had to swallow the moan that tried to claw its way up her throat.

"Talk nicely to me," he whispered against her lips.

"Why?" she gasped. "What are you going to give me in return?"

If she'd thought Robert's eyes were hard flints before, they were something wholly different now; dilated, burning pits of desire that mirrored her deepest fantasies, the ones that had been banked inside her for six months.

"Did you miss me?" he asked again.

"Yes." The word was a breathless admission, the most honest she'd ever been with a man as rich as Robert Shimizu.

"Good. Come with me," he said, backing away from her.

For a dizzying second, she felt bereft, cold, alone.

But Robert's hand never left her arm. He tightened his grip and pulled her around the registration table, deeper into the hotel. Instead of heading toward the bank of poker tables in front of them, he took a quick left toward a hidden elevator. Cleo spotted two obvious bodyguards on either side of the elevator door and another standing not so casually by, pretending to be sipping on a cocktail. When the guards saw them, one pressed the elevator call button. The doors opened and they didn't even have to stop.

They stepped inside the small elevator and Robert pressed the button to the penthouse. Even when the doors were closed, he never let her go.

"You know, this is a small elevator. You don't have to hold me so tight. Where am I going to hide?"

He turned to her and looked her up and down. She could tell that the look wasn't a consideration of the possibilities for escape; it was just because he wanted to see her and it made Cleo's mouth dry. She returned his gaze because she wanted to see him too. And suddenly she understood why he wasn't letting her go, for the same reason she'd practically pressed herself against him earlier. They both wanted to feel each other; to reassure themselves that this was real.

"Did you miss me?" she whispered to him.

His answer was to crash his mouth to hers, his soft lips prying hers open. Robert's tongue was sure as it pressed between her lips. He stroked her tongue with deep swipes, tasting every corner of her. He finally let her arm go, only to wrap his arms around her and grab her ass in a grip that was just as hard as the one on her forearm.

Cleo wrapped her arms around his neck and dug her fingers into his hair. She moaned and pulled at his silky strands.

Robert groaned into her mouth and pressed her back against the elevator wall.

She spread her legs as he settled that bulge in his pants against her mound. Cleo was in heaven when he used his grip on her ass cheeks to lift her into his arms.

"Oh fuck," she breathed, wrapping her legs around his waist.

If the elevator ride had been long enough, Cleo had no doubt that she would have fucked Robert inside it and happily. Unfortunately, as soon as the car started moving it stopped. When the elevator dinged, Robert backed quickly away from her and straightened his suit coat, his eyes narrowed in lust.

His face was smeared with a bit of her foundation and lipstick. His hair was disheveled and the fall of his pants was beautifully disturbed by his big dick. He looked perfect. He looked like hers.

"Business first," he ground out, grabbing her forearm again.

"What's second?" she asked with a playful giggle as he dragged her into his hotel room.

"What the fuck is going on?" Alex screamed in her ear.

▭

CLEO LET Robert lead her into the penthouse while Alex tried to modulate her voice to hide the way it shook with fear. This was the danger of working with her sister. The part of herself that would always be the big sister – the one who'd had to take care of her when their parents were preoccupied with her mother's slow decline and death – only wanted to shield her from all the pain and fear in the world. But she couldn't, not really, but she could take control of this moment and give her sister bread-crumbs to calm her the best way she knew how.

"Nice penthouse," she said. "I liked your house in Kentucky better."

It wasn't a lie. The penthouse was the kind of Miami luxury people paid too much money for. The open-plan living area was all oriented toward the floor-to-ceiling windows that looked out at the ocean. If someone were to look down, they could see the bustling Miami streets, and she could imagine that at night, the lights made it look like one of those fake artsy long exposure photographs white boys on Insta-gram love. But the point of the penthouse was to ignore all that and find peace in the water at the city's edge. That's why all of the furniture was faced the windows and nothing in the skyline obstructed the view. It was a beautiful, if generic, hotel room, and it would be difficult for Cleo to get the hell out of here undetected. That was one thing the Kentucky house had over this place, but it wasn't the first thing in Cleo's mind. This room was cold, fake tropical, all glass and marble tile. That house — or at least the little she'd seen of it — had been dark hard-wood, soft fabrics, lots of places to hide, lots of knick-knacks to slip in her purse, and warm. Like him.

"Okay, so this dude is from the Derby job?" Alex

whispered in her ear. "Is he the one-night stand you disappeared with?"

"Well, girl, he sounds fine, so I'm not judging you," Marcus mumbled in her ear.

"Sit," Robert said, gently pointing at a white wicker chair with a light blue throw pillow before he let her go. She missed the weight of his hand on her, but she did as he said.

He moved around the small glass coffee table to the matching seat and sat across from her. He leaned back in his chair and gracefully crossed his long legs at the knee. Cleo draped her arms across the arms of the chair and mirrored Robert's posture.

His eyes dipped to her big brown thighs. And then he grunted. That sound, after so long, did something to her body. She could feel her insides warm just watching him watch her. Her skin tingled. Her pussy was wet.

"Is this where you proposition me?" she asked him, breaking the tense silence between them.

"Yes."

"Someone better be recording this," Gina chimed in.

"Been on it since they were making out in the elevator," Brian added, voice still bored.

Cleo had to force herself not to roll her eyes. "I'm listening," she said to Robert and her trifling crew.

"Girl, us too, the fuck?" Marcus said.

"I don't want to turn you in to the police," Robert said.

"Pussy be yankin'," Marcus sang.

"Shut up," Alex hissed.

"Pussy that good?" Cleo asked.

A small smile lifted the corners of Robert's mouth. "You know it is," he said softly. "But that's not why I don't want to turn you in. I want to use you."

Had five words ever made Cleo's pussy quiver before? No. Did she have to grip the chair for a second to keep from touching herself? Absolutely. Was this man dangerous? Definitely.

She swallowed. "Use me how?" Her voice was thick with lust. Robert's smile lifted a fraction of an inch. Maybe he knew that what she'd wanted to say was, "Use me, please."

"I've been researching you and your team. How many of you are there?"

"Oh, baby," she said with a forced laugh. "There's only one me."

He rested his elbow on the side of his chair and rubbed a single finger across his lips as he stared at her, nodding contemplatively. "I agree," he whispered softly.

Cleo shivered.

"That was an audacious plan. How long did it take you to come up with it? How did you decide to hit Frank Pugh's house on the same night it was filled with hundreds of people, including a dozen highly trained security guards? Did you know you would get away, or just hope?"

"Sorry, I don't speak law enforcement."

He huffed a laugh.

"How can we strike a deal, Cleo, if you don't give a little?"

"If I remember correctly, I gave you more than a little," she said with a wicked smile as she pulled a Sharon Stone in *Basic Instinct*, uncrossing and then re-crossing her legs.

Robert's eyes didn't miss the movement.

"Use me how?" she asked again, trying to get his mind back on track and his eyes off her thighs since it was only stoking the arousal in her veins.

"Did you know I was head of security?"

"Excuse me?" she asked, sitting forward in her chair.

"He's what?" everyone on her team yelled.

"On it," Brian said.

Robert squinted at her, clearly trying to decide if her reaction was genuine. "Hmmm. That's surprising."

That wasn't the word Cleo would have used. She pushed herself up and began to pace around the periphery of the room, fuming. As soon as she got out of here, she was going to fly to wherever the hell Brian was, beat him with her favorite pair of Louboutins and implement a new requirement that every brief for future jobs include all security personnel's names *and pictures* so they'd never have this problem again.

This problem being that she might accidentally meet someone, fuck him, and then have him spend half a year looking for her. She didn't think the odds of this happening again were high — especially if she was going to jail — but she didn't think it could hurt to be too thorough.

"What's the deal?" she spat at Robert, still pacing.

"Sit," he said.

"I don't want to sit. Tell me the damn deal so I can turn you down, you can call the police and we can both move on with our lives."

"Is that what you want, Just Cleo?"

The question stopped her in her tracks. She turned to him with a frown. While she'd struggled not to blow her top and her team was scrambling to figure out what they'd gotten themselves into, Robert was still sitting calmly in his chair, his head resting against one of his fists, his eyes on her.

She watched him watch her. He reached into his pants pocket and pulled out a small piece of dark fabric. Cleo's mouth fell open, knowing in her gut what it was.

"Sit," he said again. His voice was deeper than it had been just a second ago. Harder. And it made her wetter. It made her mouth dry. It made her want to do things she shouldn't, like call him Mr. Shimizu again. But she couldn't do that, so she sat back in her chair, this time with a stiff back and her arms crossed over her chest.

"I want to know what you know," he said calmly, his thumb stroking the fabric of her underwear.

"What does that mean?"

"It means, I threw this party to get you here, but not so I can turn you in. I want you to tell me how you planned to work a party like this and all the other ways you might run a con here. I want to know what you know so I can do my job better."

Cleo frowned at him. She hadn't spent six months secretly hoping for a job offer. This wasn't what she wanted. But if it got her out of this mess — and got Alex as far away from danger as possible — she had to at least entertain it. "So hypothetically, I tell you how to prepare your henchmen against a criminal mastermind — which I'm not, just in case we're being recorded," Robert smiled and nodded, "and then you just let me go?"

Something... hot flashed behind his eyes. "Come here?"

"Sit. Come. Man, I'm not a dog," she said.

He frowned quickly and leaned forward, her underwear clutched in his fist. "You're not. And that's not how I want to make you feel," he said, his deep voice caressing her skin.

Cleo's nipples hardened painfully. "How do you

want to make me feel?" she asked before she could stop herself. She watched as Robert uncrossed his legs and spread them obscenely, his erection obvious and mouthwatering.

"Come here and I'll show you."

She didn't think, and that was a bad sign. Cleo needed to figure out a way to get out of here, but that didn't matter when Robert looked at her like he was and spoke to her like he had and the way he'd made her feel six months ago. She stood from her chair, walked around the coffee table and stopped in between his spread legs.

As soon as she was within arm's reach, Robert sat up straight and placed his bare hands just behind her knees.

Cleo gasped. She couldn't have stopped the exhalation of breath even if she'd tried, because it wasn't just about this one touch. Robert's hands landing softly on her most sensitive patch of skin broke the seal on six months of desperation. Six months of wondering where he was, what he was doing, and if he was thinking about her. Six months of missing him; of wanting him to touch her in just this way and so many others.

His eyes were trained on her face, watching her eyes widen, tracking her tongue as she licked her heavily painted lips. His fingers skimmed up the back of her legs, under the hem of her dress and then back again, feather light.

She twitched at that touch. "Is that my thong?" she asked, needing to be sure.

"It is," he said, "I've kept it with me ever since you left." He sat back in his chair, leaving his lap open in invitation for her.

Cleo didn't hesitate to hike up her dress — he grunted — and straddle his legs.

Robert pulled her fully into his lap, settling her ass over his erection. They both moaned at that contact.

"I need a moment," she said, ripping her earpiece from her ear.

Robert lifted an eyebrow. "Your crew?"

"No idea what you're talking about."

He smiled. "You didn't answer my other question."

"Which question was that? There's been a few."

"Do you want us to just walk away from each other and go on with our lives?"

"Are you offering something different?" she asked, but she was too scared to hear the answer so she decided to distract him. Cleo ran her hand between his legs, palmed his erection, and leaned down to kiss him quickly.

Or at least she'd planned to distract him.

Robert's hands moved to her wrist and her neck.

Cleo ground her sex against his dick and groaned at his tight hold on her again.

He moved her hand from his erection and placed

it over his heart. She opened her palm and felt his heartbeat pounding against his chest. Her eyes flew to his.

"I spent six months trying to find you; I think it's clear that there's more."

"I'm listening," she whispered.

"You ran away," he said.

"That's not an offer."

"Stay with me."

Cleo licked her lips and ground against his dick again. "Is that an offer or a command?"

Robert smiled. "Can I command you to stay? Is that a thing you'd do?"

"Maybe."

"I want you to stay with me," he said, but didn't command. Cleo found that frustrating, but she wasn't sure exactly why.

"Is that the deal? I agree to stay with you and then you don't call the cops?"

"No. You help me tie up cracks in my crew and I forget everything I've learned about your... profession in the past few months. But you decide where you go after that. *If* you go."

"My team," she said.

"Your team, if you have one, isn't my concern. Just you," he whispered, tightening his hold on the back of her neck and pulling her face down to his. "You said it the night we met. Just Cleo. I only want you."

ROBERT HAD SPENT months dreaming of this moment. Of Cleo's tongue in his mouth and his hand crawling up her inner thigh.

His stomach clenched at the warmth between her legs and his ears burned at the soft whimpers falling from her lips. He moved two fingers over her wet underwear. He wanted her wetter. He reluctantly released her neck to move his palm down her back. He squeezed her ass and her whimpers turned to moans as she pressed her pussy down onto his fingers.

He pressed her underwear between her slit, circling her clit. "Ride my fingers," he commanded.

"Yes, Mr. Shimizu," she whispered.

He grunted and squeezed her ass again, thrusting his hips up toward her.

Her hips began to move in slow circles as she rode the palm of his hand. Their eyes were locked to one another's. Cleo's gaze was burning, fierce. He wondered how he'd survived so long without her.

"It could be like this from now on," he whispered to her. "You could go straight."

"Sounds boring," she said.

He moved his fingers inside the gusset of her underwear and slipped two fingers into her pulsing cunt.

Her head fell back with a loud cry.

"This feel boring to you, sweetheart?"

"Oh fuck," she screamed. Her body shuddered in his arms and her pussy clenched around his digits.

He squeezed her ass again, encouraging her to ride his fingers harder and faster. "We could spend every day and night together. I can give you whatever you want. You won't have to steal a thing. But if you need the rush, you can take everything I have. Just stay with me." His voice was wild, hoarse, desperate. Robert had never had to plead for a thing in his life, but Cleo was worth it; worth more than this, actually.

He thrust his hips up at her while she circled her hips down onto his fingers. The room was full of the sounds of Cleo's desperate cries, Robert's grunts and the chair scraping against the marble as they rutted against one another. He'd never heard anything so beautiful.

"Look at me," he demanded.

She did so immediately, moving her hands to clutch his shoulders, nails digging into his jacket. She whimpered and moaned. "I'm close," she whined.

"Stay with me," he begged. His dick was painfully hard, and he wanted nothing more than to undo his pants and replace his fingers with his shaft. But he needed an answer. He'd made himself a promise somewhere along the way that when he finally got inside Cleo again, he wanted it to be forever. He wanted to be able to take his time with her, get reacquainted with every part of her body. He wanted to chart any changes with his tongue. He wanted to remind her of what it felt like to be in his control. And then he wanted to fall asleep knowing that he wouldn't have to worry about waking up without her again. He needed that. They deserved that.

"Cleo," he barked.

"Can I come?" she screamed. "Please, let me come."

"Answer me," he said.

She was riding his fingers wildly now. She moved her hands to bracket his face, watching him as she tried to stop herself from letting the orgasm take her over. "Please," she whined.

"Please," he echoed.

He could see it, just on the tip of her tongue. He was certain that she'd been just about to tell him yes.

But then the fire alarm began to blare in the room.

And they both lost it.

EIGHT

THE FIRST THING Cleo thought when her muscles relaxed and she shuddered a breath, blinking back into consciousness after an orgasm that made lights flash behind her eyelids, was, "Mr. Shimizu is going to be pissed I came without approval," and she'd shivered in anticipation. The second thing she thought was that she hadn't felt as peaceful as she did in that moment in too long to remember. And the third thing she thought was that someone needed to turn that fucking alarm off because it was fucking up her post-orgasmic high.

"Cleo," Robert murmured against her chin. His beard was so soft and downy against her skin that she was rubbing against it like some kind of attention-starved cat. "We have to get out of here," he whispered against her jaw.

She wanted to tell him not yet. That this was probably just a false alarm. But she just kept snuggling into his arms, rubbing her face against his beard, probably covering him with her makeup, and letting herself feel the rightness of that.

Then the elevator behind them dinged and some strange man Cleo didn't recognize burst into the room. "Let's get a move on," he said.

Cleo came fully into consciousness and frowned at him. "We're busy. Who the fuck are you?"

The man looked down at her with amused eyes for a second before turning to Robert. "I guess I can see why you spent a fucking fortune looking for her." And then he turned back to Cleo. "Thanks for the overtime. Now, get a move on."

Cleo balked.

"Calm down," Robert whispered to her.

His voice was lighter than she'd ever heard. He sounded... happy. She turned to him and saw the truth of that in his eyes.

"They'll clear the hotel and then we'll come back."

"What about the charity poker games?"

He shrugged. "Stevie'll handle that," he said, motioning toward the man beckoning them to what must be an emergency exit door on the far side of the room.

"I'm not walking down thirty flights of stairs."

"Not with that attitude," Stevie called. "Let's go."

"We only have to go down three flights then we can cross to the north wing of the hotel. Come on."

She stood from his lap in a huff. Her knees were weak and her inner thighs were sticky. She moved so Robert could stand and shimmied her dress from around her waist. *Alex is going to kill me*, she thought to herself. That made her remember that she'd taken out her earpiece and her eyes darted around the floor at her feet.

"Looking for this?" Robert asked, his palm open to her.

Cleo's eyes lifted to his, and his gaze wasn't soft and warm anymore. He was looking at her as if he was trying to figure out a puzzle. That was smart, if not also terrifying.

She snagged her earpiece from his palm and held it delicately between two fingers. "I—"

"Let's. Fucking. Go," Stevie called from the emergency exit.

"Tell me later," he said and grabbed her other hand, a lot of emphasis on that final word.

Cleo let him pull her toward the exit as she slipped her earpiece back on.

"Cleo. Cleo, what's happening? What the fuck is going on?"

"Sounds like he's sweating her wig glue off, but I don't know," Gina said nonchalantly.

"At least fucking up her makeup a little bit," Marcus said.

"Shut the fuck up. Cleo," Alex called again.

"I'm here," she muttered.

Alex didn't hide her sigh of relief. "Thank god. Here's the plan."

Cleo held onto Robert's hand as he led her down the three flights of stairs at a brisk but careful pace, his eyes on her heels, she noticed. She followed him out onto the twenty-seventh floor, where a steady stream of security seemed to be ushering people through the fire doors and across the elevated walkway to the north tower. The walkway was clear all around and Cleo, who wasn't particularly afraid of heights, made the mistake of looking down. Below them, the city just kept moving, as if the drama in this hotel didn't mean anything. She moved her free hand to the hand joined with Robert's and leaned into his side.

"I've got you," he muttered to her on instinct, squeezing her palm in his.

Halfway to the north tower, another man fell into step next to Robert. Cleo assumed he was another of his employees because he started to give him a rundown.

"Seems like it's a false alarm. Maybe a prank. But the fire department has to come through and clear each floor. You want us to set you up in the other penthouse?"

Robert shook his head. "No, that's fine. Where's the hotel manager?"

"Across the way. We got him up here to meet with you."

"Good."

Cleo didn't have a hard time following their conversation while also listening to her sister tell her what to do. What kind of criminal would she be if she couldn't multitask?

When they made it through the other set of fire doors, Cleo saw a group of people heading to the fire stairs on this side of the hotel. In the opposite direction, she saw a group of men in suits and tactical gear — clearly Robert's security — surrounding a small, balding man she guessed was the hotel manager.

They stopped walking and Robert turned to her. "Wait here. This'll only take a minute."

Cleo did not believe in gushy sentimentality. She didn't mind emotion, but dramatics? Not her bag. That's why she surprised even herself when she pulled Robert's face to hers, shoved her tongue in his mouth and kissed the fuck out of him.

He grabbed onto her waist immediately, pulling her body to his. No hesitation. She'd never had that before. "I'll be right back," he whispered. "Tomas'll stay with you," he said, nodding to the man who'd joined them in the walkway.

She nodded. "Hurry back."

He brushed his mouth against hers one more

time, and then he and Stevie turned away. She watched him, but only for a few seconds. Alex's plan was too flimsy, with no margin for error. She turned quickly to Tomas.

"Is there a bathroom on this floor?" she asked, even though she knew there wasn't.

He shook his head and then spoke into a two-way speaker clipped to his shirt. She saw Stevie turn toward them, but she didn't turn his way. If she did, he might have seen something in her eyes that she so rarely felt: regret. She kept her eyes trained on Tomas and waited as he spoke quickly back and forth with Stevie.

"There's one on the next floor down. Follow me," he said.

Cleo nodded quickly and joined Tomas as he stepped into the line of guests heading to the stair-well. Just before she walked through the door, she turned her head. She caught one last glimpse of Robert; hands on his hips, his head bent as he listened to the hotel manager speak. His hair was partially obscuring his face. She'd remember him like this forever, she thought sadly.

As she was looking away, her eyes clashed with Stevie's. She didn't know him well enough to recognize the look in his eyes but she turned away, stepping into the stairwell quickly. She didn't know what Stevie had seen in her eyes, but she decided to imagine that this plan had even less time for execution than before, and maybe she'd already made the gravest error she could imagine: she looked back.

She followed Tomas down a flight of stairs. He pulled the door to the hallway open for her. She sighed. *He must be new at this*, she thought to herself. *That's useful.* The hallway in front of them was deserted.

"Bathroom's over there," he said, indicating a door close to the elevator.

"Don't you need to check it?" she asked.

"For what?"

Cleo frowned and shrugged. "I don't know. But I'm sure Mr. Shimizu would want you to be very diligent with me." Then she smiled at him and waited.

If he were close to Robert or had been doing this longer than a second, he'd have told her that there wasn't a threat here, she could pee in peace. But Cleo could read people — well, most people — and she'd figured Tomas correctly.

His eyes darted around the hallway and then to the bathroom door. "Stay here," he said to her.

"Obviously. I need to piss. Be quick."

He frowned and then walked to the bathroom. As soon as the door closed, she pressed the elevator call button. The doors opened immediately and Cleo slipped through them as soon as she could.

"'Bout time," Marcus said with a broad smile.

They both pressed the button to close the doors on either side of the elevator. Cleo didn't let herself breathe until the elevator doors closed again.

"He'll know I'm gone before we even get to the lobby," she said, her eyes riveted on the illuminated numbers as they descended.

"Oh, def. Brian said your man is worth a cool hundred mill. Old money and new money. Contacts in the FBI and some spy agency I've never heard of? I don't know."

She turned to Marcus and he smiled at her like he always did, as if nothing serious was really happening and danger was an illusion. "Good thing we're getting off before then."

She squinted at him. "Alex said the getaway's through the lobby."

"Did she?" Marcus asked, pressing his lips shut.

On the fifth floor, the elevator stopped. Marcus leaned out into the hallway to make sure their path was clear. Cleo followed him down the hall to the vending area. There was a service elevator back here and the doors opened as soon as they pressed the call button.

"In," Marcus said. Cleo heard him next to her and through her earpiece.

"Good," Alex said. "There's a cargo van at the rear service entrance. License plate AHX 1090. Mississippi plates. Keys are in the ignition."

"Got it," Marcus said.

Cleo kept waiting for something or someone to impede their exit; maybe one of Robert's bodyguards, maybe just regular hotel security, or hell, maybe even just a police officer wondering what the hell they were doing in the employees only areas.

But nothing happened.

If Robert knew that she was gone, he hadn't been able to get his men to the service areas in time to stop them. If his men were scouring the property, they were looking for a tall Black woman in a pastel pink wig running away on foot, not a light-skinned man in a bellhop uniform driving a beat-up gray van. And as Cleo knew, a job well done was all in the details and Robert didn't have any of them.

Cleo sat on a bench in the back of the van as Marcus drove them away. She turned to look out of the back windows and watched the hotel recede into the distance. She didn't know what to do with the grief she felt welling in her chest the farther away the car moved, so she channeled her emotions into anger.

Because Robert wasn't the only one who didn't know all the details.

MARCUS DROPPED Cleo off across town at the hotel where she and Alex were staying.

"I'll get rid of the car then get out of town."

Cleo nodded numbly.

"You okay?" he asked, his smile slipping.

"I'm fine," she said. She wasn't. "You should get out of town, like now."

His smile brightened again. "Oh yeah, duh. Actually, my girl was pissed at me 'cause I was supposed to take her to Mexico for New Year's. Bought the tickets and everything, but I had to cancel for this job. But since this ain't work out, I can head home, scoop her up and not have her pissed off at me as we try and start some new shit."

Cleo smiled.

"That's what they say, you know?"

"What's what they say?"

"On New Year's Eve. You're supposed to get your home and your life in some kinda order. You only want to take your best intentions into the New Year. And that's my intention, not to piss my girl off for no reason. So I guess I should thank you. Happy New Year, Cleo."

"Happy New Year, Marcus. See you next year."

He winked at her and then pulled away from the curb.

Cleo felt like she was in a daze as she rode the elevator up to the suite she and her sister shared. Alex pulled the door open as soon as she knocked and then pulled her inside, hugging her.

"I'm so fucking pissed at you," Alex muttered into Cleo's hair.

Cleo wrapped her arms around her sister. "I'm fine. I'm here."

Alex stepped back, her face furious. "Right. You're here, not in jail, because of me. Not because of you. Because if it was up to you, you'd be fucking that moneybag in the penthouse. You'd be letting that mark get you off."

Cleo could have denied her sister's accusation, but she hated lying to Alex. She always had. They were sisters, best friends, and partners. There wasn't any room for lies, not in their line of work, and not with their history.

Cleo had never really gotten a choice about whether or not Alex tagged along on her heists. Even before her mother had gotten sick, her dad had always told her that the two of them were a team. In fact, she could just almost remember her dad putting baby Alex in her arms and telling her that it would be the two of them against the world. And when he started spending more time at the hospital than at home, he'd impressed upon Cleo that she had to look after Alex until their mom was better. She'd never gotten better and Cleo had never stopped looking after Alex and now, her sister was looking after her.

"What the fuck happened back there, Cleo?" Alex asked. "Who the fuck was he?"

Cleo kicked her shoes off and walked into their suite, Alex hot on her heels.

"He's the guy from Kentucky."

"Got that. So, it wasn't just a one-night stand?" she asked accusatorily.

Cleo spun around. "No, it was. I haven't seen him in six months."

"Bullshit," she hissed, squinting at Cleo. "Right?"

Cleo shook her head and began to chew on her bottom lip.

"What the fuck happened that night?"

"I don't know," Cleo admitted truthfully. "It was just supposed to be sex. It was the best fucking sex of my life, but I-I don't know. It was something else too."

"Something else like what?"

Cleo didn't know, so she pivoted. "How long do you think we can do this?"

"Do what?"

"Scam. Steal. Live like the only thing that matters is the next job."

"Girl, what? You were just telling me barely even a few hours ago that this job was so important we shouldn't take a fucking vacation. Now this random ass man gives you an orgasm and you're talking about retirement."

Cleo started chewing her lip again.

"Do you really want to quit?" Alex whispered, her face crestfallen, her voice wounded.

It broke Cleo's heart.

She could still remember her and Alex's first boost together.

She was twelve. Alex was nine. It was summer and their mom hadn't been feeling good for weeks. Dad was going to take her to the hospital and Cleo was heading out the front door to go meet her friends at the park across the street. Their dad had stopped her and told her that wherever she was going, Alex was going too; whatever she was getting into, Alex was getting into as well.

Now, of course he'd meant some real wholesome shit, like she needed to share the television at night. Or if she had a candy bar, she needed to give Alex a piece, as usual. And if they were playing kickball in the park, Cleo had to pick Alex to be on her team. But as it happened, on that day, Cleo and her little hoodrat friends had been making plans; they were going to rob their local corner store. And when they shoved single packs of top ramen and popsicles down their baggy pants, Alex had been right there, a cute nine-year-old with a missing front tooth and raggedy pigtails; the perfect distraction.

If she'd known then she was creating a monster... well, she still would have done it, because Alex was a natural and Cleo's plan had been incomplete without a decoy, but she would have definitely thought twice about bringing her type-A little sister into this lifestyle long term. Not because she was ashamed of her job, but because having your baby sister all in your ear when you're trying to get shit done was hard as fuck. And having her see right through you made it damn hard to run from the truth.

"Yeah," Cleo heard herself say. "I think I'm done." And then she was laughing, feeling a lightness in her chest she hadn't known was possible. "Bitch, I love you, but I'm out."

NINE

NEW YEAR'S EVE

Kentucky

ROBERT THOUGHT about sleeping in his office. Not on purpose, of course, or at least that's what he would have told himself. His brain would have concocted some story about just *needing* to get the stack of contracts signed, returned and filed before the new year. Or he might have opened the bar, the bar he usually only used for clients, just so he could justify staying at work so he didn't add to the already unsafe New Year's Eve traffic.

But he hadn't gotten the chance to do any of those things.

Just as he'd been staring at the decanter of vodka on top of the bar, he'd gotten a call from his neighborhood security.

"Hello," he barked in a voice raspy from disuse.

"Hello, Mr. Shimizu. This is Ernest from the Hillcrest Community Security Force. We got word from your home security provider that there was a break-in at your house."

"Okay."

"So... we went and checked it out."

"And?" Robert asked, getting annoyed.

"And we just wanted to tell you that we haven't found any evidence of a break-in."

Robert rolled his eyes. "Okay. Thanks. Goodbye."

"Wait," Ernest said. "It's Hillcrest policy that when there aren't any obvious signs of an intruder but there's been an alarm notification, residents should double-check that all is well."

"Okay. I'll do that when I can."

"Speedily," Ernest added.

Robert sighed and rolled his eyes again. "Fine. I'm on my way."

"Thank you, sir."

Robert hung up the phone.

His eyes darted to the bar again and he shook his head. He stood from his desk, thought about shoving the remaining contracts into his bag but changed his mind. He'd go home, check his house and return to the office as soon as possible. And he practically chanted that to himself on the short drive home.

When he pulled into his driveway, there was a security guard standing at his front door. He smiled and waved at Robert, and then probably remembered what Robert did for a living before pulling up his utility belt and straightening his back.

Robert had to take a deep breath before he pushed his car door open.

His eyes darted up the façade of his house to his bedroom window and then away as quickly as possible. For the past two weeks, he'd done everything he could to be away from home as much as possible so he could avoid his bedroom. For six months his bed had been like a sanctuary to that one night with Cleo, but after Miami, it had become a place of mental torture.

All the images of the night after the Derby haunted him as they mingled with the way she'd looked down at him while riding his hand and that last look before she'd run away again. He could excuse the first time, neither of them had really known how it could be between them. But the second time... she'd known. She'd felt it. He knew that because he'd felt her feel it. Those few seconds before the fire alarm had gone off, he'd seen the look on her face and he'd known that she was about to say yes.

At least that was the lie he was able to tell himself when he stayed away from the bedroom where she'd ruined him for other women only to refuse to keep him, even when he'd begged her to do just that.

Robert slammed the car door behind him, took another deep breath and then forced his face into a smile. "Hello, Ernest, right?" he asked, because his foul mood wasn't this man's fault.

"Yes. Yes, sir. I'm sorry to inconvenience you, but protocol."

"Of course," Robert said.

The man followed Robert to his front door. Robert only hesitated for a second before he unlocked the door and pushed it open.

That tiny voice in his head that had screamed at him since the night he'd met Cleo had gone quiet since Miami. Sometimes he rejoiced in his newfound quiet, even as he'd mourned the loss. But when he stepped into his home, that voice sighed sadly; it had been hoping that maybe... It was wrong again. He'd been wrong about Cleo once again.

"Is everything okay?" Ernest asked. "Anything out of place?"

Robert looked around his large living and dining room. All his big expensive possessions were present and accounted for, and nothing looked out of place. If someone had broken in, he couldn't see any signs of it, but he also found himself not caring, because it all looked wrong to him, because Cleo wasn't here. "It's fine. Everything's fine," he said, turning to the front door. He forced himself to smile.

Ernest seemed relieved. "You sure? You don't

want to check upstairs or the garage? I can come in and help."

Robert shook his head. "That won't be necessary." But he did walk across the kitchen to check the garage so the man would leave him to grieve in peace.

He had to take a deep breath in and push it out loudly before he could open the door. Much like his bedroom, Robert had come to associate the garage with Cleo. She had stolen his Jag. But it wasn't the memory of his favorite car that made him avoid his garage; it was the memory of Cleo's wary eyes and soft voice saying, "Kiss me," and the phantom feeling of her lips against his.

It didn't make any sense. Cleo hadn't spent more than a few hours here, and yet Robert felt as if every square inch of his home was haunted by her. And when he opened the garage, he thought at first that what he was seeing was just an extension of his mind's refusal to let him forget her. But the longer he stared, the more he started to believe that this was real.

He stepped into his garage and put his hand on the hood of his car. It was just slightly warm.

"Everything okay?" Ernest called from the front door.

Robert turned back to his house. His entire body felt as if he'd been hit with a high volt of electricity as he shut his garage door and walked back through the kitchen.

"Yep. Yeah," he said. His voice sounded strange. Too high. He didn't care. "Everything's great. Thank you for calling me and... doing your job so well."

Ernest's entire face lit up. "You're welcome. If you notice anything, just give us a call."

Robert nodded, already closing the front door. "Of course."

"Have a good evening, and Happy New Year, Mr. Shimizu," he said quickly.

"Happy New Year to you as well," he replied, his heart racing.

He turned to look at his home anew. Everything was in its place as it had been before, but it all looked different, or at least Robert suddenly thought it did. His eyes darted left and right, looking for any sign of her. That sad voice in his head had returned and was practically chanting at him to find her now, now, now, and for once, he listened to it without hesitation.

He took the stairs two at a time. His eyes zeroed in on his closed bedroom door at the end of the hall and he ran toward it, not caring that it made him seem desperate; he was. He stopped just outside his bedroom, certain the door had been open when he'd left this morning, but once again unsure if his pathetic brain and heart were making this up.

His hand closed slowly around the doorknob and he pushed it down and pressed forward.

The door opened to his bed — a bed he hadn't been able to sleep in since he'd returned from Miami — and there she was, sitting cross-legged in the middle of his bed, completely naked, his father's watch on her wrist.

"Finally. I didn't have time to turn your air down. I'm cold as fuck," Cleo said, a gorgeous mask of annoyance on her face.

CLEO TRIED to look confident even though her stomach was doing flips.

She'd had two weeks to plan this reunion since she'd left her sister fuming in Miami. She could have gone directly back to the Grand Palace and found Robert, but Cleo thought there was a chance he might have changed his mind about calling the police, so she headed back to Chicago to sweeten the deal.

She'd thought about off-loading his car. She could have gotten a lot of money for it, but each time she thought to call the chop shop she used to move her automobiles, she couldn't do it. She'd never planned to sell the watch, especially not when she saw the name *Calvin Shimizu* engraved on the back. Clearly, it was his father's, and it was a sentimental piece. She never thought about returning it though, because it was something that connected them; an intimate bond he didn't know she'd cherished.

In Chicago, she'd stopped by her dad's house, told him to take it easy on Alex if she seemed annoyed in the next few months, and hit up her contacts to have the car transported back to Kentucky. She'd waited an agonizing few days, staking out his gated community until his car had arrived. And then she'd broken into his house. Cleo had never robbed a house in reverse, and it sucked. She couldn't imagine anything that was the exact opposite of the rush she was looking for.

But then Robert had pushed his bedroom door open and she changed her mind. Giving him back his possessions was okay. Staring down a foreseeable future where she *didn't* lift some rich woman's Gucci purse carelessly abandoned on the department store counter while she looked for another tacky purse to waste money on? Grim. But if it meant that Robert looked at her like this — wide eyes, heaving chest, slightly disheveled hair, beard full and lush like the softest seat she'd ever seen, his body coiled tight like he was about to pounce...that might be just the kind of incentive she'd need to adjust to getting out of the game and starting something new. With him.

"You just gonna stare at me?" she asked in a small whisper.

That got him moving. He stepped into the room

with a stuttered step, as if he'd forgotten how to walk on two legs. Cleo couldn't blame him, she looked fucking great. She'd practiced this pose in the mirror over the past week more than a few times in various hotel rooms across the Midwest. She'd felt awkward each time, but she'd also wanted this moment to be perfect. She wanted the first time Robert saw her after Miami and six months after the Derby to be memorable. And what was more memorable than her, butt ass naked except for his watch and a brand-new lavender wig that matched her fresh manicure?

Nothing.

"You're here?" he said as he stalked around the bed.

"In the flesh," she said, leaning back on her hands, following him with her eyes.

His eyes narrowed. "Why are you here?"

A lesser person's face would have fallen at that not-quite-welcome response. But Cleo was used to awkwardness, so she took it in stride, even though her heart felt as if it was breaking. "I've got a proposition for you," she said.

"No," he spat before she could finish speaking and practically launched his body onto the bed, crawling on top of her.

"Don't you want to hear—" she tried to ask, as he pushed her flat on her back.

"No," he said again. He grabbed her wrists and

extended them over her head, holding them in one hand.

When he moved his free hand to grip her throat, Cleo couldn't help but exhale, her entire body going slack under his, relaxed.

But Robert only seemed to stiffen on top of her, his grip on her wrist and neck tightening and his dick hardening in his pants. Cleo spread her legs so that bulge could settle against her core where it belonged.

"Why are you here?" he whispered again.

Cleo rolled her eyes. "I was trying to tell you."

He unconsciously thrust his hips, and she purred at the friction of his groin grinding into her bare pussy. She felt the rage rolling off of him and into her in waves and it made her smile.

"Don't smile," he barked, thrusting with each word.

Cleo moved her head forward and licked his lips. "No."

"Why are you here?" he asked again.

"Don't you want me here?" she asked, arching her back to rub her breasts against his chest.

"You left me." Robert's voice broke and his eyes looked so sad and tired. Cleo's smile faltered.

"Can I trust you?" she asked.

He scoffed. "Can *you* trust *me*?"

It wasn't a real question, but she treated it as such. "Yes. Can I trust you not to call the police?"

"Yes," he said immediately.

"I don't care what you do to me, but my crew..." She swallowed and took a deep breath. "I had to protect my sister."

"Your...? You work with your sister?" His hands loosened and he lifted from her body. The cool air of the bedroom covered her chest and she missed the warmth of him.

Even just thinking about Alex made her eyes water, but she shook her head, wanting to change the subject. "Worked," she corrected, lowering her eyelashes — her real ones this time, she hadn't wanted to risk this man ruining another pair of her favorite real mink wispies.

He squinted down at her.

"I retired."

She felt his grip on her tighten again. "When?" His voice was hoarse with barely contained emotion.

Cleo relaxed in his hold, finally feeling the ice between them begin to really thaw. "Two weeks ago."

"Miami?" he asked in desperation.

"Miami," she confirmed.

"What now?" he asked, his head unconsciously dipping, his mouth getting closer to hers.

Cleo smiled and shrugged while she wrapped her legs around his waist and locked her ankles behind his ass. "I could do so many things now."

"Like what?"

She licked her lips and shimmied, shamelessly rubbing her naked body against his soft wool suit.

"Like what, Cleo?" he repeated, his voice a deep sonorous whisper so full of possibility it made her core clench.

"I heard you were looking for a consultant."

"I'm not."

Her eyebrows lifted. "You're not?"

He shook his head. "A consultant is temporary. I need something more permanent." He dipped his head, nuzzling her jaw with his nose.

"Yeah?"

"Yes, Cleo," he whispered against her lips as his head moved to the other side of her jaw to repeat the nuzzling there. He was teasing her and she wasn't mad at it.

She bit her bottom lip, pretending to consider his words. "I think that can be arranged," she moaned.

His head lifted. His eyes danced with mirth for a brief moment before they deadened. "How do I know I can trust you? How do I know you won't just leave again?"

She hadn't known what to expect of this reunion, but she'd been prepared for this question. Cleo turned her head to look at his watch on her left wrist. "I've never returned anything I've stolen before. Never got caught." She turned to him with wide eyes. "I'm not ashamed of what I do. What I did. But it didn't make me as happy as it used to. It never made me feel as much as you did in that car and this room." She lifted her head from the bed toward him and he lowered to meet her halfway. "Ask me to stay," she whispered against his lips.

"Will you stay with me?"

"Yes," she said, and he pressed his mouth to hers in a brief but hard kiss.

"Now, ask me the other thing," she said, and snapped his mouth between her teeth gently.

He kissed her first. He flattened his body against her, ground his dick against her pussy, tightened his fingers around her throat. "How do you want to be punished?"

Cleo had never shivered harder in her life. "I don't stay where I'm not wanted. I want you to make me stay. Make me *want* to stay."

"Have you ever stayed put before?"

Cleo smiled, loving how clearly he could already see her. "Never," she whispered.

"Neither have I," he said, his hips pumping against her.

She smiled and moaned low in her throat, digging her heels into his ass trying to get him closer, inside her. He moved his hand from the front of her neck, down her chest. He palmed her right breast and then strummed her nipple with his thumb.

Her head felt back to the bed and she sighed.

"Stay with me," he mumbled against her cheek,

not as a request or a command, but almost like a prayer.

Cleo smiled, snuggling into his beard.

"Do you like that?" he asked, rubbing his beard across her skin.

She moaned.

He stopped moving, his face buried in her neck, but without the hot friction of his hair against her skin.

She frowned. "Don't stop."

He didn't answer.

Cleo was getting frustrated, but then she felt the soft press of his lips against her shoulder. She could feel his smile.

She sighed and rolled her eyes. "Yes, Mr. Shimizu. I love the way your beard feels against my skin, Mr. Shimizu. Please don't stop, Mr. Shimizu," she trilled, her voice laced with sarcasm. "Asshole," she muttered under her breath.

"Good girl," he whispered into her ear, shaking with laughter. "Now I know how to punish you."

"Wait. Hold up. How?"

He didn't listen. Cleo started squirming underneath him as he scraped his beard over her naked body, sometimes softly, sometimes so hard it almost hurt. When he rubbed his beard over her nipples, the scratching of his hair was interspersed with flicks of his tongue and the scraping of his teeth.

"Oh fuck," she groaned.

He lifted from her body and she arched her back, wanting his touch back, even when it hurt.

"Keep your hands above your head," he growled.

She nodded excitedly. "Yes, sir. Now get to work."

Robert shook his head while he rolled his eyes. But instead of getting down to business on her body, he sat back on his haunches and began to take his tie off.

"Motherfucker," she hissed.

"I told you to speak nicely to me and I'd give you whatever you want."

"I was nice! I'm butt ass naked! How much nicer do I need to be?"

He'd started unbuttoning his shirt while she whined. Cleo thought that the more unhinged she felt as her lust grew, the calmer Robert looked. And it might have been frustrating in the moment, but actually, it was sexy as fuck.

"Please," she moaned.

"That's better," Robert said as he ripped his belt open and fished his dick from his pants.

Cleo spread her legs wider and smiled. "I missed you," she whispered to his dick.

"Ridiculous," Robert said, and then he fisted his dick and began to jack himself off on top of her.

Cleo's mouth fell open on a gasp. "You better fucking not," she screamed.

ROBERT GRUNTED and his dick jerked in his hand. She was so beautiful angry. And haughty. And scared. And annoyed. Cleo was perfect. "Do not move your hands," he told her.

He let go of his dick briefly to stick two fingers into her pussy. They both groaned. She was even wetter and warmer than he remembered. He pumped his fingers into her and moved the thumb from his other hand to circle her clit.

Cleo planted her feet on the bed and jutted her hips up to him, begging him to fill her, touch her, taste her. And he would. Robert had six months of fantasies to play out with Cleo and he was certain she had a few of her own. He doubted they'd leave this room for a good long while. He couldn't think of a better way to ring in the new year than in this bed, working Cleo over with everything he had and doing exactly as she'd asked; giving her more than a few reasons to stay.

She was close. Her thighs shook with her coming orgasm and the effort to keep her hips raised. He bent over and took a greedy lick of her clit. She cried out and then shuddered when he slapped her wet clit lightly with the pads of his fingers.

"Yes," she breathed.

And then he stopped.

Her ass fell to the bed. "Nooo," she whined, looking down at him.

He grabbed his dick again with the hand wet from her pussy and started masturbating again.

"Bitch," she hissed.

"Is that nice?"

"It's as nice as you're going to get."

He lifted an eyebrow. "Is it?" he asked, gripping the head of his dick with his other hand and squeezing as he stroked his length.

Cleo licked her lips and then pressed her thighs together. Robert watched as the ghost of an orgasm ran through her. She shivered, her eyes closed as a soft moan escaped her lips. "Please," she whispered in the sweetest moan of desperation.

Robert grunted, his control practically disintegrated. He pushed Cleo's knees apart and then pushed into her with a single press of his hips. He didn't give her time to adjust to the intrusion and he felt certain that if he'd tried, she might have resorted to violence.

Instead, he grabbed her hips and pulled her up to the perfect angle to pump into her as deep as possible, as hard as possible.

He fucked her with six months of pent-up lust and frustration and she fucked him back with the same. He looked down at her body — her breasts swaying with the force of their bodies moving, her mouth open on a perpetual moan and, best of all, her hands clutched together above her head — not wanting to disobey him.

"You're perfect," he panted.

"I know. Now please," she begged, fucking him back.

His mouth watered at the hard points of her nipples. He let her back down to the bed and moved his hands across her stomach and up her ribs. He tickled the undersides of her breasts softly before grabbing them and squeezing, just hard enough that she would feel the bite.

Her muscles locked. Her thighs held him. Her pussy clenched and she came in a wet gush so strong, she pushed his dick out of her pussy.

"Please," she ground out.

He shoved his dick back inside her and began to fuck her again, fucking her just as fast and just as hard. She was bucking underneath him so he covered her body with his own trying to hold her down. He moved his face back to her breasts and began to suckle and bite at her nipples while using his beard to drive her wild. She was screaming at the top of her lungs. Robert had never heard a sound so perfect.

She was close again, he could feel it, but he didn't let up on her. He sucked her nipple into his mouth and caressed it with his tongue before biting lightly. She shuddered and came, and he fucked her through that release and then another. And another.

By the time he covered her body fully with his, fucking her into the mattress, he was gritting his teeth trying to keep his orgasm at bay.

"Stay," he grunted.

"Come," she replied.

And so he did.

His hips jerked as he emptied inside her. His lips met hers and he groaned his relief into her mouth. She met each press of his body against hers happily.

When he was spent, he collapsed onto her and she wrapped her legs and arms around him.

"You didn't ask me if you could come," he mumbled against her lips, unwilling to stop kissing her after so long apart.

"You said I could steal from you if I needed the thrill," she laughed.

Robert wrapped his arms around her body and held her tight. "I meant my money or my cars."

She shrugged in his hold. "Been there. Done that," she said, shaking with laughter.

Robert watched her, tears falling from her eyes as she laughed at her own joke. He heard the faint sound of fireworks in the distance and he smiled. He dipped his head and brushed his lips over the rounded tip of her nose, and then across the high points of each cheekbone. He kissed the corner of her mouth and then her lips. "I wonder if you'll be laughing when I'm rubbing my beard all over your pussy. No fingers, no dick, no tongue," he said, the threat delivered in his most gentle voice.

Cleo's face sobered and she opened her eyes to look up at him. "Yes, please, Mr. Shimizu," she whispered.

He smiled at her and lifted back onto his knees.

Her hands went over her head again, fisting the comforter beneath her. He kissed his way down her body, his eyes trained on hers as she watched him descend. Robert pressed a soft kiss against her engorged clit. She jumped.

His tongue was out and he was ready to taste her when she stopped him with an arched eyebrow.

"Your security is terrible. You didn't even change your garage opener."

"I wanted you to come back," he whispered.

"I'm sorry I stole your father's watch."

"It's just a thing. So is the car. I wanted *you* to come back. Just you," he said, and lowered his mouth to her sex, set on making sure she knew that he didn't just want her here, he needed her.

"MR. SHIMIZU WILL BE right in. Can I get you something to drink?" Mr. Shimizu's personal assistant asked.

Kierra looked quickly around the large office. It was heavy with dark woods, and a large window on the north wall that shone light only on the large desk at the center of the room, casting the rest of the space in shadow. She, Monica, and Lane moved in front of the three hardbacked chairs facing the desk, and she sat in the middle, putting the cute new soft briefcase she'd bought to seem more professional on the low table in front of them.

Monica looked at the young man and smiled. "No, thank you. We're fine."

"Actually," Kierra said, holding up her index finger. "Do you have sparkling water?"

"Of course. What flavor would you like?"

"What flavors do you have?" she asked excitedly.

Monica huffed in annoyance and Kierra smiled wider, waiting for Mr. Shimizu's assistant to answer her question.

"We have lime, lemon, blackberry, orange, and plain, of course."

"Blackberry sounds good," Lane said, leaning slightly to his left, closer to Kierra.

"I think so too," she said. "Can we," she gestured between herself and Lane, "have blackberry, please?"

"Of course." His gaze shifted to Monica. "Are you certain I can't get you something?"

Kierra shifted in her seat and turned to Monica. She felt Lane shift behind her, probably to look at Monica as well.

Monica rolled her eyes at them and looked at the assistant. "Lemon, please."

"Coming right up," he said and walked briskly from the room.

"That wasn't so hard, was it?" Kierra asked Monica.

Monica rolled her eyes again. Lane chuckled softly.

"Did you have to wear that skirt?" Monica asked, her eyes falling not to Kierra's skirt but her bare thighs. They stayed there.

Kierra batted her eyelashes. "I like it, and it was a Christmas present from Lane."

"I had it made specially for her. And it matches

your suit," he said, nodding at Monica's perfectly tailored pinstripe pantsuit.

Monica lifted her eyes and glared at them. Kierra shivered and licked her lips.

"It's too short," Monica said.

"That's not what you said when I tried it on last week, not that I got to keep it on for long," she purred.

"That's my point exactly," Monica said.

Her face looked bored, completely uninterested in this mundane conversation. But Kierra knew her better than that. She recognized the slight squinting of her eyes and the way she pursed her lips; it was one of her favorite expressions on Monica's face. She was trying to suppress her desire because they were in public. Kierra didn't care where they were, that look was worth it every time.

"I said you could come only if you behaved," Monica said. "We don't technically need you to be in this meeting."

"I know. But technically, this is an important instructional opportunity." She leaned toward her. "And you never expressly defined what you meant by 'behave.'"

Lane's laughter was bright and happy, and it made Kierra shiver again. "Well, she's got you there."

The office door opened. Kierra didn't turn her head while the assistant returned with their drinks. Instead, she kept her eyes on Monica as she crossed her right leg over her left and "accidentally" knocked Monica's thigh with the toe of her knee-high suede boot – another gift from Lane – with a raised eyebrow.

"Is there anything else?" the assistant asked.

"Oh no," Lane said. "We're good."

When the man had left again, Monica reached out to put her hand on Kierra's thigh.

Kierra's mouth fell open in a big, excited smile. "I realize that you two think this is funny."

"Because it is," Lane said, pulling the tab on his can of sparkling water.

"Anything could happen when we're in the field."

"Like a Serbian dictator putting out a hit on me?" Kierra offered.

"Or worse. Much worse. And you know that." Monica's eyes flitted briefly away from Kierra's to Lane.

If Lane was chastened, Kierra couldn't feel it, but she was. She shifted in her seat and sat up straight, looking forward. There were only a few seconds of silence before Monica's hand squeezed her thigh and then shifted higher up her leg, her pinky just brushing the hem of Kierra's admittedly — and purposely — very short skirt.

Monica leaned over their chairs and brushed her lips against Kierra's cheek. "I just want to keep you safe, sweet girl," she whispered into Kierra's ear. "I don't know what we'd do if anything happened to you."

Kierra's body was hot, but not from arousal. Or not *only* from arousal. She turned to Monica and smiled her biggest smile. "You two wouldn't let anything happen to me," she said earnestly. "And Maya would make sure that Kenny avenged me if something did."

"What about us? We wouldn't avenge you?" Lane asked, his arm moving to the back of her chair. Kierra's eyes closed when she felt his mouth press against her hair, kissing her.

"If something happens to me, it's because something happened to you two. I'm safest when we're all together."

Monica smiled, but it was small and worried, and her eyes looked sad. Kierra wanted to kiss that look away, or sit on it, but she exercised the tiny bit of restraint she possessed and just grabbed Monica's hand on her leg and squeezed.

"Besides, Lane's been helping me with my weapons training," she said brightly.

"That's actually the most dangerous thing I've ever done. I'd be worried about that."

Kierra turned to him. "It was an accident," she huffed. "And I made it up to you."

Lane brushed his lips across her mouth. "Yeah, you did."

A door behind the desk opened swiftly, and a

tall, skinny man in a severe dark suit walked into the room. His hair was just past his shoulders, and it fluttered as he walked briskly around his desk. Kierra's eyebrows rose in interest.

"Monica," he said, extending his hand in greeting.

"Robert," Monica said, as she stood and shook Mr. Shimizu's hand with the hand that had just been holding Kierra's leg. "This is my husband and partner, Lane."

Lane stood and shook hands, and then they all turned to Kierra, still sitting; shivering.

"And this is Kierra, our..."

Kierra's eyes moved to Monica, waiting for her to finish that sentence.

Monica's eyes danced with mirth, and Kierra much preferred that to sadness.

"Associate," Monica finished.

"That's one word for it," Lane muttered.

Kierra stood and extended her hand to Mr. Shimizu.

"Nice to meet you," he said, and then bent over to brush his mouth across the back of her hand.

"I like him," Kierra breathed.

Mr. Shimizu stood, and they all chuckled politely, while Kierra continued to stare at him, mesmerized.

"Please, sit," he said, and then walked back around his desk.

"Behave," Monica mouthed as they sat back down.

"You didn't say he was hot," Kierra hissed, and turned to frown at Lane. "She never said he was hot."

Lane patted her knee and winked at her. "Take it out on her later," he whispered.

"So," Mr. Shimizu cut into their quiet argument, "what can I help you with?"

Monica was all business now. She extended her hand to Kierra, who was a little annoyed, so it took her a quick second to realize what was happening.

"Oh, sorry," she said, and then pulled the file folder from her bag and placed it in Monica's hand. Lane squeezed her knee reassuringly.

Monica stood and placed the file folder on Mr. Shimizu's desk and then walked back to her seat. "We've been assigned to look into a string of bank heists across Western Europe."

Mr. Shimizu's eyebrows lifted as he reached for the folder.

"The basic MO is that a small but very efficient and very capable crew of people gain access to the safety deposit boxes and then clean out *only* the ones with either precious jewelry or large amounts of foreign currency. They're so good that most of the people who own the boxes don't even know they've been hit until anywhere from three to six months later. We think."

"Think?" Mr. Shimizu asked, looking at Monica over the edge of the folder.

"We've been unable to confirm the exact dates of the robberies."

"They're that good?"

"Better," Lane interjected. "What you have in front of you is a collection of security footage from four of the *dozen* banks we've been able to trace the crew to, or at least we think it's the same crew. We can't be sure. In fact, we're not even sure if the woman in the photographs is the same woman. But we know that around the times the banks think they've been hit, a beautiful and very tall Black woman visited under the pretense of legitimate business."

Mr. Shimizu put the folder down on his desk and looked at them with sympathetic eyes. "The Agency doesn't usually come to me with such thin information."

"True," Monica conceded. "But as you can tell, we've hit a wall. Some of our associates were investigating the robberies, but the crew went underground."

"Because of the investigation?"

"Maybe. We don't even know that. What little we know is that this woman might be involved or might not. She might know something of interest."

"Or she might not," Mr. Shimizu added.

"She might not," Lane echoed.

"How can I help you?"

"Do you recognize the woman in the pictures?" Monica asked.

Mr. Shimizu huffed a small laugh and looked at the images. "These are some of the worst security images I've ever seen." He looked at them again, shuffling them around and then shook his head. "But no, I don't recognize this woman."

"Are you sure?" Monica asked.

"I am. But we can ask my new associate." He pressed a button on his phone. "Troy, can you send her in, please?"

"Yes, sir."

"New associate?" Monica asked.

Kierra recognized the tiniest hint of warning in her voice. If Mr. Shimizu noticed, it didn't ruffle him, and Kierra thought that was a feat. He was either very dumb and unable to sense danger, or he was a bigger badass than Kierra initially thought. If it was the latter, she thought that was sexy as fuck. She turned her head to whisper that to Lane when the office door opened and a woman entered.

"Holy shit, fuck me," Kierra breathed.

Lane and Monica's heads turned and then tilted back.

The woman who walked into the office was tall, maybe even taller than Mr. Shimizu, and thick everywhere. Kierra's eyes widened as she took her in from the top of her head and her bone-straight black hair with dark purple tips. She, not unlike Kierra, was dressed just barely professionally in the tightest jumpsuit. It was unbuttoned to show off a lovely expanse of chest. Kierra thought it would be unprofessional to try and get a little glimpse of cleavage, but she angled her head to the side, nonetheless. There was a thin belt around her waist that cinched her in and accentuated the flare of her hips, drawing Kierra's eyes to her thighs and then down her thick legs to her tall, open-toed snakeskin heels.

"Yes, sis," Kierra muttered under her breath.

They watched as the woman walked across the office behind Mr. Shimizu's desk. The man pushed his chair back and looked up at the new woman, smiling when she bent down to kiss him chastely on the cheek.

"This is my new associate," he said, turning back to see them all slack-jawed. "This is my wife, Cleo. Cleo, these are some of my... associates, from The Agency."

"What agency?" she asked, with a lifted, perfectly arched eyebrow.

"That's the name," Lane offered, "just The Agency."

Cleo frowned at him. "Sounds fake."

Kierra nodded. "Very."

"But it's not," Mr. Shimizu said. "The Agency is an international... intelligence agency."

"Close enough," Monica replied.

"They're here asking for my help with a series of bank robberies. Do you recognize this woman?"

Cleo's eyes moved to the desk and she bent forward to rifle through the photographs.

Kierra also bent forward, or at least she tried to but Monica put her hand on Kierra's arm and pushed her back. Kierra frowned at her.

"Behave," Monica mouthed again.

"Nope. Sure don't," Cleo said.

Kierra turned back to the desk and watched as Mr. Shimizu wrapped his arm around Cleo's thighs and she leaned into him.

"I'm sorry we couldn't be of more help," he said.

"So am I," Monica said. "But if you come across any information, The Agency would appreciate it."

Mr. Shimizu nodded once. Cleo pressed a button on his phone and the office door opened again. "Troy will show you out."

They stood, and Kierra grabbed her briefcase. She and Cleo locked eyes, and the woman smiled at her and then winked. Kierra smiled back. Lane reached out and grabbed one of her hands, and Monica put a firm hand at the small of her back. They followed Mr. Shimizu's assistant to the elevator. He pressed the button and then ushered them inside. He stepped into the elevator and rode down to the lobby with them, and then pushed open the front door, smiling kindly at them as they exited.

Out in the parking lot, Kierra squinted at the

bright sunlight, only just realizing how dark Mr. Shimizu's office had been.

"So, his wife is the bank robber, right?" she blurted out.

Lane turned to her and laughed. "Hell fucking yeah." He pressed a button on the key fob to unlock their car and opened the back door for her.

"So, what are we going to do about it?" she asked, stopping in her tracks.

Monica turned to her. "Nothing. For now."

"Why? Don't we want to close this case?"

Lane shrugged. "We were asked to contact our sources. We did."

"And he lied to us. Right to our faces," Kierra exclaimed.

"He did. But the robberies have stopped," Monica said.

"But—"

"Instructional note number whatthefuckever," Lane said, as he wrapped an arm around her waist and pulled her to him. "Some sources are more important than the job. These robberies aren't our main priority, and Robert Shimizu has contacts in security all over the world. We need to protect that relationship more than we need to report back to our bosses that his new wife *used* to get into a little bit of robbing. Allegedly."

"But—"

Monica stepped close to them and brushed Kierra's hair behind her right ear. "And if his new wife is the woman in the photographs, she has contacts that might prove *very* useful to us in the future. When we don't tell The Agency, Robert will owe us a very large favor in the future, and that man always pays his debts. This is a short-term failure to ensure a long-term success. Remember that, Kierra."

Kierra looked back and forth between them with wide eyes, and then frowned at Lane. "Did you see her shoes?"

His entire face lit up. "I did. There's a mall nearby, how 'bout we do a little shopping?"

Monica rolled her eyes and walked around to the passenger seat. "You two are insufferable."

Lane smiled down at Kierra and then kissed her on the tip of her nose. "She says that like she don't like it."

Kierra laughed as she slipped into the back of the car. As Lane drove them from the parking lot, her eyes lifted up to the tall building counting the tinted glass, trying to figure out which window was Mr. Shimizu's. She wondered if he and Cleo were watching them drive away.

CLEO SLID onto Robert's desk, right on top of the security images of her in Geneva and Berlin and Manchester and Paris.

"You think they know it's me?" she asked.

He ran his index finger across his lips and grunted. She knew that grunt; it meant yes, but also that he wanted to fuck her.

His eyes were focused on the buttons of her jumpsuit and she smiled, loving watching him watch her. She moved her right hand to the belt at her waist and pulled at one of the sides, so it fell open. Then she moved both hands to the third button of her jumpsuit and unbuttoned it. He watched her with the kind of focus that she'd once been afraid she'd never find in a man, and had even been terrified would wane the longer they were together. It had only been six months, but if anything, that concentration had only intensified with each day.

She unbuttoned another button, and an errant ray of light from the uncovered window caught on the ridiculously large diamond wedding ring Robert had chosen, not just because it was worth a large mansion, but because it was sentimental. When he'd presented the uncut diamond to her, he'd given her the slip of sale from the auction of the estate of Mr. Francis Pugh III. She'd been so overcome with emotion she couldn't say yes to his proposal until they woke up hungover — from whiskey and sex — in the middle of the next day.

Her hands stilled on the button covering her navel. "Do you think they're going to turn me in?" she asked.

His eyes lifted to hers and seared into her. Robert's hands moved to her thighs and rubbed up and down before he gripped them and stood from his chair. Then he covered her hands with his own and undid that button, and then the next one.

Cleo moaned as he slipped his hand inside her jumpsuit and into her underwear. She leaned back to give him more room to gently stroke her clit, his eyes on her the entire time.

"No," he finally said, "I don't think they'll turn you in. But if they do, I don't have any problem taking them down to keep you safe."

Cleo smiled up at him, her eyes hooded and her breath panting. "Yes, Mr. Shimizu," she said with a smile.

ACKNOWLEDGMENTS

I have an overactive imagination and this story is the product of that, so if you've made it this far I just want to thank you for spending a few hours in my odd brain lol, I really do appreciate it! Thanks Kai for inundating my DMs with random pictures of celebrities you know I like, almost like you're throwing darts at the wall of my imagination and seeing what sticks. And this STUCK! If any readers enjoyed watching Cleo and Robert be dirty and a little emotional, but you're sad for Alex, don't be! Cleo might have left the game, but her little sister's still out there, robbing and scamming but completely unaware that she'll meet her matches soon enough. And if you don't know who Monica, Kierra and Lane are, but think you might be into married spies who are *very* into their personal assistant, you can pick up Pink Slip on Amazon!

Getting through the random writing phase for this project was difficult. I lost someone I love a lot and it was hard for me to focus on much besides my grief some days, but there were some really kind people who helped me through, even if they didn't know it. Thank you Chencia C. Higgins for reading this foolishness and encouraging me to... keep writing it! And thank you so much to Tasha L. Harrison, Lucy Eden and Zaida Polanco for being so supporting and pushing me to like "be better" or whatever, even when I just wanted to sleep and chat. And I guess thanks to my cats for once again yelling at me and cuddling me while I grieved. Y'all might not pay any bills but I guess you contribute to the household in other ways. And if you're reading this, thank you, for encouraging me this year, reading my stories, recommending them, thirsting with me on twitter, and just being yourself; it all meant so much to me.

If you liked this story, please consider leaving a review wherever you feel most comfortable. And even better, if you know someone who might like this story, I'd love it if you would recommend it to them. 2019 was a strange year of lots of ups and downs but I was brought to tears so many times by how many of you told me you liked my stories and recommended them far and wide. You'll never know what that means to me. Thank you and happy new year! <3

The Family

Beautiful & Dirty

The Hitman

Bay Area Blues

Layover

Back in the Day

Heist Holidays

Grand Theft N.Y.E.

Standalones

Encore

Office Hours

The Tenant

Sex Toy Soldier